Henry James

The Madonna of the Future and Other Tales

Vol. II

Henry James

The Madonna of the Future and Other Tales
Vol. II

ISBN/EAN: 9783337030391

Printed in Europe, USA, Canada, Australia, Japan

Cover: Foto ©Andreas Hilbeck / pixelio.de

More available books at **www.hansebooks.com**

THE

MADONNA OF THE FUTURE.

AND OTHER TALES.

BY

HENRY JAMES, JR.

IN TWO VOLUMES.

VOL. II.

London:

MACMILLAN AND CO.

1879.

LONDON :

R. CLAY, SONS, AND TAYLOR,

BREAD STREET HILL.

CONTENTS OF VOL. II.

EUGENE PICKERING.

THE MADONNA OF THE FUTURE,

AND OTHER TALES.

EUGENE PICKERING.

I.

IT was at Homburg, several years ago, before the gaming had been suppressed. The evening was very warm, and all the world was gathered on the terrace of the Kursaal and the esplanade below it, to listen to the excellent orchestra; or half the world, rather, for the crowd was equally dense in the gaming-rooms, around the tables. Everywhere the crowd was great. The night was perfect, the season was at its height, the open windows of the Kursaal sent long shafts of unnatural light into the dusky

VOL. II.   B

woods, and now and then, in the intervals of the
music, one might almost hear the clink of the
napoleons and the metallic call of the croupiers rise
above the watching silence of the saloons. I had
been strolling with a friend, and we at last prepared
to sit down. Chairs, however, were scarce. I had
captured one, but it seemed no easy matter to find a
mate for it. I was on the point of giving up in
despair and proposing an adjournment to the silken
ottomans of the Kursaal, when I observed a young
man lounging back on one of the objects of my
quest, with his feet supported on the rounds of
another. This was more than his share of luxury,
and I promptly approached him. He evidently
belonged to the race which has the credit of knowing
best, at home and abroad, how to make itself comfortable ; but, something in his appearance suggested
that his present attitude was the result of inadvertence rather than of egotism. He was staring at the
conductor of the orchestra and listening intently to
the music. His hands were locked round his long legs,
and his mouth was half open, with rather a foolish
air. " There are so few chairs," I said, " that I must
beg you to surrender this second one." He started,

stared, blushed, pushed the chair away with awkward alacrity, and murmured something about not having noticed that he had it.

"What an odd-looking youth!" said my companion, who had watched me, as I seated myself beside her.

"Yes, he is odd-looking ; but what is odder still is that I have seen him before, that his face is familiar to me, and yet that I can't place him." The orchestra was playing the Prayer from *Der Frei-schütz*, but Weber's lovely music only deepened the blank of memory. Who the deuce was he ? where, when, how, had I known him ? It seemed extraordinary that a face should be at once so familiar and so strange. We had our backs turned to him, so that I could not look at him again. When the music ceased we left our places, and I went to consign my friend to her mamma on the terrace. In passing, I saw that my young man had departed ; I concluded that he only strikingly resembled some one I knew. But who in the world was it he resembled ? The ladies went off to their lodgings, which were near by, and I turned into the gaming-rooms and hovered about the circle at roulette. Gradually, I filtered

through to the inner edge, near the table and, looking
round, saw my puzzling friend stationed opposite
to me. He was watching the game, with his hands
in his pockets ; but singularly enough, now that I
observed him at my leisure, the look of familiarity
quite faded from his face. What had made us
call his appearance odd was his great length and
leanness of limb, his long, white neck, his blue, pro-
minent eyes, and his ingenuous, unconscious ab-
sorption in the scene before him. He was not
handsome, certainly, but he looked peculiarly
amiable ; and if his overt wonderment savoured a
trifle of rurality, it was an agreeable contrast to
the hard, inexpressive masks about him. He was
the verdant offshoot, I said to myself, of some ancient,
rigid stem ; he had been brought up in the quietest
of homes, and he was having his first glimpse of life.
I was curious to see whether he would put anything
on the table ; he evidently felt the temptation, but he
seemed paralysed by chronic embarrassment. He
stood gazing at the chinking complexity of losses and
gains, shaking his loose gold in his pocket, and every
now and then passing his hand nervously over his
eyes.

Most of the spectators were too attentive to the play to have many thoughts for each other; but before long I noticed a lady who evidently had an eye for her neighbours as well as for the table. She was seated about half way between my friend and me, and I presently observed that she was trying to catch his eye. Though at Homburg, as people said, "one could never be sure," I yet doubted whether this lady were one of those whose especial vocation it was to catch a gentleman's eye. She was youthful rather than elderly, and pretty rather than plain ; indeed, a few minutes later, when I saw her smile, I thought her wonderfully pretty. She had a charming grey eye and a good deal of yellow hair disposed in picturesque disorder ; and though her features were meagre and her complexion faded, she gave one a sense of sentimental, artificial gracefulness. She was dressed in white muslin very much puffed and frilled, but a trifle the worse for wear, relieved here and there by a pale blue ribbon. I used to flatter my-self on guessing at people's nationality by their faces, and, as a rule, I guessed aright. This faded, crumpled, vaporous beauty, I conceived, was a German—such a German, somehow, as I had seen imagined in litera-

ture. Was she not a friend of poets, a correspond-
ent of philosophers, a muse, a priestess of æsthet-
ics—something in the way of a Bettina, a Rahel?
My conjectures, however, were speedily merged in
wonderment as to what my diffident friend was making of her. She caught his eye at last, and raising
an ungloved hand, covered altogether with blue-
gemmed rings—turquoises, sapphires, and lapis—she
beckoned him to come to her. The gesture was
executed with a sort of practised coolness and accompanied with an appealing smile. He stared a
moment, rather blankly, unable to suppose that the
invitation was addressed to him; then, as it was immediately repeated with a good deal of intensity, he
blushed to the roots of his hair, wavered awkwardly,
and at last made his way to the lady's chair. By the
time he reached it he was crimson, and wiping his
forehead with his pocket-handkerchief. She tilted
back, looked up at him with the same smile, laid two
fingers on his sleeve, and said something, interrogatively, to which he replied by a shake of the head.
She was asking him, evidently, if he had ever played,
and he was saying no. Old players have a fancy
that when luck has turned her back on them, they

can put her into good-humour again by having their
stakes placed by a novice. Our young man's physiognomy had seemed to his new acquaintance to
express the perfection of inexperience, and, like a
practical woman, she had determined to make him
serve her turn. Unlike most of her neighbours, she
had no little pile of gold before her, but she drew
from her pocket a double napoleon, put it into his
hand and bade him place it on a number of his own
choosing. He was evidently filled with a sort of
delightful trouble ; he enjoyed the adventure, but he
shrank from the hazard. I would have staked the
coin on its being his companion's last ; for, although
she still smiled intently as she watched his hesitation, there was anything but indifference in her pale,
pretty face. Suddenly, in desperation, he reached
over and laid the piece on the table. My attention
was diverted at this moment by my having to make
way for a lady with a great many flounces, before
me, to give up her chair to a rustling friend to whom
she had promised it ; when I again looked across at
the lady in white muslin, she was drawing in a very
goodly pile of gold with her little blue-gemmed
claw. Good luck and bad, at the Homburg tables,

were equally undemonstrative, and this happy adventuress rewarded her young friend for the sacrifice of his innocence with a single, rapid, upward smile. He had innocence enough left, however, to look round the table with a gleeful, conscious laugh, in the midst of which his eyes encountered my own. Then, suddenly the familiar look which had vanished from his face flickered up unmistakably; it was the boyish laugh of a boyhood's friend. Stupid fellow that I was, I had been looking at Eugene Pickering !

Though I lingered on, for some time longer, he failed to recognise me. Recognition, I think, had kindled a smile in my own face; but, less fortunate than he, I suppose my smile had ceased to be boyish. Now that luck had faced about again, his companion played for herself—played and won, hand over hand. At last she seemed disposed to rest on her gains, and proceeded to bury them in the folds of her muslin. Pickering had staked nothing for himself, but as he saw her prepare to withdraw, he offered her a double napoleon and begged her to place it. She shook her head with great decision, and seemed to bid him put it up again; but he, still blushing a good deal, pressed

her with awkward ardour, and she at last took it from
him, looked at him a moment fixedly, and laid it on
a number. A moment later the croupier was raking
it in. She gave the young man a little nod which
seemed to say, "I told you so"; he glanced round
the table again and laughed; she left her chair,
and he made a way for her through the crowd. Before going home I took a turn on the terrace and
looked down on the esplanade. The lamps were out,
but the warm starlight vaguely illumined a dozen
figures scattered in couples. One of these figures, I
thought, was a lady in a white dress.

I had no intention of letting Pickering go without
reminding him of our old acquaintance. He had been
a very singular boy, and I was curious to see what had
become of his singularity. I looked for him the next
morning at two or three of the hotels, and at last I
discovered his whereabouts. But he was out, the
waiter said; he had gone to walk an hour before. I
went my way confident that I should meet him in
the evening. It was the rule with the Homburg
world to spend its evenings at the Kursaal, and
Pickering, apparently, had already discovered a good
reason for not being an exception. One of the

charms of Homburg is the fact that of a hot day
you may walk about for a whole afternoon in un-
broken shade. The umbrageous gardens of the
Kursaal mingle with the charming Hardtwald, which
in turn melts away into the wooded slopes of the
Taunus Mountains. To the Hardtwald I bent my
steps, and strolled for an hour through mossy glades
and the still, perpendicular gloom of the fir-woods.
Suddenly, on the grassy margin of a by-path, I came
upon a young man stretched at his length in the
sun-checkered shade and kicking his heels towards a
patch of blue sky. My step was so noiseless on
the turf, that before he saw me, I had time to recognise Pickering again. He looked as if he had been
lounging there for some time; his hair was tossed
about as if he had been sleeping ; on the grass near
him, beside his hat and stick, lay a sealed letter.
When he perceived me he jerked himself forward,
and I stood looking at him without introducing
myself—purposely, to give him a chance to recognise
me. He put on his glasses, being awkwardly near-
sighted, and stared up at me with an air of general
trustfulness, but without a sign of knowing me. So
at last I introduced myself. ' Then he jumped up

and grasped my hands and stared and blushed and laughed and began a dozen random questions, ending with a demand as to how in the world I had known him.

"Why, you are not changed so utterly," I said ; "and after all, it's but fifteen years since you used to do my Latin exercises for me."

" Not changed, eh ? " he answered, still smiling, and yet speaking with a sort of ingenuous dismay.

Then I remembered that poor Pickering had been in those Latin days a victim of juvenile irony. He used to bring a bottle of medicine to school and take a dose in a glass of water before lunch ; and every day at two o'clock, half an hour before the rest of us were liberated, an old nurse with bushy eyebrows came and fetched him away in a carriage. His extremely fair complexion, his nurse, and his bottle of medicine, which suggested a vague analogy with the sleeping-potion in the tragedy, caused him to be called Juliet. Certainly, Romeo's sweetheart hardly suffered more ; she was not, at least, a standing joke in Verona. Remembering these things, I hastened to say to Pickering that I hoped he was still the same good fellow who used to do my Latin

for me. " We were capital friends, you know," I
went on, " then and afterwards."

" Yes, we were very good friends," he said, " and
that makes it the stranger I shouldn't have known
you. For you know as a boy I never had many
friends, nor as a man either. You see," he added,
passing his hand over his eyes, " I am rather dazed,
rather bewildered at finding myself for the first time
—alone." And he jerked back his shoulders nervously and threw up his head, as if to settle himself
in an unwonted position. I wondered whether the
old nurse with the bushy eyebrows had remained
attached to his person up to a recent period, and
discovered presently that, virtually at least, she had.
We had the whole summer day before us, and we sat
down on the grass together and overhauled our old
memories. It, was as if we had stumbled upon an
ancient cupboard in some dusky corner, and rummaged out a heap of childish playthings—tin soldiers
and torn story-books, jack-knives and Chinese puzzles.
This is what we remembered between us.

He had made but a short stay at school—not
because he was tormented, for he thought it so fine
to be at school at all that he held his tongue at

home about the sufferings incurred through the medi-
cine-bottle ; but because his father thought he was
learning bad manners.   This he imparted to me in
confidence at the time, and I remember how it increased my oppressive awe of Mr. Pickering, who
had appeared to me in glimpses as a sort of high-
priest of the proprieties.   Mr. Pickering was a
widower—a fact which seemed to produce in him
a sort of preternatural concentration of parental
dignity.   He was a majestic man, with a hooked
nose, a keen, dark eye, very large whiskers, and
notions of his own as to how a boy—or his boy,
at any rate—should be brought up.   First and fore-
most, he was to be a "gentleman " ; which seemed
to mean, chiefly, that he was always to wear a muffler
and gloves, and be sent to bed, after a supper of bread
and milk, at eight o'clock.   School-life, on experiment, seemed hostile to these observances, and
Eugene was taken home again, to be moulded into
urbanity beneath the parental eye.   A tutor was
provided for him, and a single select companion was
prescribed.   The choice, mysteriously, fell on me,
born as I was under quite another star ; my parents
were appealed to, and I was allowed for a few

months to have my lessons with Eugene. The tutor, I think, must have been rather a snob, for Eugene was treated like a prince, while I got all the questions and the raps with the ruler. And yet I remember never being jealous of my happier comrade, and striking up, for the time, one of those friendships of childhood. He had a watch and a pony and a great store of picture-books, but my envy of these luxuries was tempered by a vague compassion which left me free to be generous. I could go out to play alone, I could button my jacket myself, and sit up till I was sleepy. Poor Pickering could never take a step without asking leave, or spend half an hour in the garden without a formal report of it when he came in. My parents, who had no desire to see me inoculated with importunate virtues, sent me back to school at the end of six months. After that I never saw Eugene. His father went to live in the country, to protect the lad's morals, and Eugene faded, in reminiscence, into a pale image of the depressing effects of education. I think I vaguely supposed that he would melt into thin air, and indeed began gradually to doubt of his existence and to regard him as one

of the foolish things one ceased to believe in as
one grew older. It seemed natural that I should
have no more news of him. Our present meeting
was my first assurance that he had really survived
all that muffling and coddling.

I observed him now with a good deal of interest, for
he was a rare phenomenon—the fruit of a system
persistently and uninterruptedly applied. He struck
me, in a fashion, as certain young monks I had seen
in Italy; he had the same candid, unsophisticated
cloister-face. His education had been really almost
monastic. It had found him evidently a very com-
pliant, yielding subject; his gentle, affectionate spirit
was not one of those that need to be broken. It had
bequeathed him, now that he stood on the threshold
of the great world, an extraordinary freshness of impression and alertness of desire, and I confess that, as
I looked at him and met his transparent blue eye, I
trembled for the unwarned innocence of such a soul.
I became aware, gradually, that the world had already
wrought a certain work upon him and roused him to
a restless, troubled self-consciousness. Everything
about him pointed to an experience from which he
had been debarred ; his whole organism trembled

with a dawning sense of unsuspected possibilities of feeling. This appealing tremor was indeed outwardly visible. He kept shifting himself about on the grass, thrusting his hands through his hair, wiping a light perspiration from his forehead, breaking out to say something and rushing off to something else. Our sudden meeting had greatly excited him, and I saw that I was likely to profit by a certain overflow of sentimental fermentation. I could do so with a good conscience, for all this trepidation filled me with a great friendliness.

"It's nearly fifteen years, as you say," he began, "since you used to call me 'butter-fingers' for always missing the ball. That's a long time to give an account of, and yet they have been, for me, such eventless, monotonous years, that I could almost tell their history in ten words. You, I suppose, have had all kinds of adventures and travelled over half the world. I remember you had a turn for deeds of daring ; I used to think you a little Captain Cook in roundabouts, for climbing the garden fence to get the ball, when I had let it fly over. I climbed no fences then or since. You remember my father, I suppose, and the great care he took of me ? I lost him some five months ago. From those boyish days up to his death we were always together. I don't think that in fifteen years we spent half-a-dozen hours apart. We lived in the country, winter and summer, seeing but three or four people. I had a succession of tutors, and a library to browse about in ; I assure you I am a tremendous scholar. It was a dull life for a growing boy, and a duller life for a young man grown, but I never knew it. I was perfectly happy." He spoke of his father at some length, and with a respect which I privately declined to emulate. Mr. Pickering had been, to my sense, a frigid egotist, unable to conceive of any larger vocation for his son than to strive to reproduce so irreproachable a model. "I know I have been strangely brought up," said my friend, "and that the result is something grotesque; but my education, piece by piece, in detail, became one of my father's personal habits, as it were. He took a fancy to it at first through his intense affection for my mother and the sort of worship he paid her memory. She died at my birth, and as I grew up, it seems that I bore an extra-ordinary likeness to her. Besides, my father had

a great many theories; he prided himself on his
conservative opinions; he thought the usual Ameri-
can *laisser-aller* in education was a very vulgar
practice, and that children were not to grow up
like dusty thorns by the wayside. So you see,"
Pickering went on, smiling and blushing, and yet
with something of the irony of vain regret, "I am
a regular garden plant. I have been watched and
watered and pruned, and if there is any virtue in
tending I ought to take the prize at a flower-show.
Some three years ago my father's health broke down,
and he was kept very much within doors. So, although I was a man grown, I lived altogether at
home. If I was out of his sight for a quarter of an
hour he sent some one after me. He had severe
attacks of neuralgia, and he used to sit at his window,
basking in the sun. He kept an opera-glass at hand,
and when I was out in the garden he used to watch
me with it. A few days before his death, I was
twenty-seven years old, and the most innocent youth,
I suppose, on the continent. After he died I missed
him greatly," Pickering continued, evidently with no
intention of making an epigram. "I stayed at home,
in a sort of dull stupor. It seemed as if life offered

itself to me for the first time, and yet as if I didn't know how to take hold of it."

He uttered all this with a frank eagerness which increased as he talked, and there was a singular contrast between the meagre experience he described and a certain radiant intelligence which I seemed to perceive in his glance and tone. Evidently he was a clever fellow, and his natural faculties were excellent. I imagined he had read a great deal, and recovered, in some degree, in restless intellectual conjecture, the freedom he was condemned to ignore in practice. Opportunity was now offering a meaning to the empty forms with which his imagination was stored, but it appeared to him dimly, through the veil of his personal diffidence.

"I have not sailed round the world, as you suppose," I said, "but I confess I envy you the novelties you are going to behold. Coming to Homburg you have plunged *in medias res.*"

He glanced at me to see if my remark contained an allusion, and hesitated a moment. "Yes, I know it. I came to Bremen in the steamer with a very friendly German, who undertook to initiate me into the glories and mysteries of the fatherland. At this season, he said, I must begin with Homburg. I landed but a fortnight ago, and here I am." Again he hesitated, as if he were going to add something about the scene at the Kursaal; but suddenly, nervously, he took up the letter which was lying beside him, looked hard at the seal with a troubled frown, and than flung it back on the grass with a sigh.

"How long do you expect to be in Europe?" I asked.

"Six months, I supposed when I came. But not so long—now!" And he let his eyes wander to the letter again.

"And where shall you go—what shall you do?"

"Everywhere, everything, I should have said yesterday. But now it is different."

I glanced at the letter interrogatively, and he gravely picked it up and put it into his pocket. We talked for a while longer, but I saw that he had suddenly become preoccupied; that he was apparently weighing an impulse to break some last barrier of reserve. At last he suddenly laid his hand on my arm, looked at me a moment appealingly, and cried, "Upon my word I should like to tell you everything!"

"Tell me everything, by all means," I answered, smiling. "I desire nothing better than to lie here in the shade and hear everything."

"Ah, but the question is, will you understand it? No matter; you think me a queer fellow already. It's not easy, either, to tell you what I feel—not easy for so queer a fellow as I to tell you in how many ways he is queer!" He got up and walked away a moment, passing his hand over his eyes, then came back rapidly and flung himself on the grass again. "I said just now I always supposed I was happy; it's true; but now that my eyes are open, I see I was only stultified. I was like a poodle-dog that is led about by a blue ribbon, and scoured and combed and fed on slops. It was not life; life is learning to know one's self, and in that sense I have lived more in the past six weeks than in all the years that preceded them. I am filled with this feverish sense of liberation; it keeps rising to my head like the fumes of strong wine. I find I am an active, sentient, intelligent creature, with desires, with passions, with possible convictions—even with what I never dreamed of, a possible will of my own! I find there is a world to know, a life to lead, men and women to form a

thousand relations with. It all lies there like a great
surging sea, where we must plunge and dive and feel
the breeze and breast the waves. I stand shivering
here on the brink, staring, longing, wondering,
charmed by the smell of the brine and yet afraid of
the water. The world beckons and smiles and calls,
but a nameless influence from the past, that I can
neither wholly obey nor wholly resist, seems to hold
me back. I am full of impulses, but, somehow, I am
not full of strength. Life seems inspiring at certain
moments, but it seems terrible and unsafe; and I ask
myself why I should wantonly. measure myself with
merciless forces, when I have learned so well how to
stand aside and let them pass. Why shouldn't I turn my
back upon it all and go home to—what awaits me?—
to that sightless, soundless country life, and long days
spent among old books? But if a man *is* weak, he
doesn't want to assent beforehand to his weakness; he
wants to taste whatever sweetness there may be in
paying for the knowledge. So it is that it comes back
—this irresistible impulse to take my plunge—to let
myself swing, to go where liberty leads me." He
paused a moment, fixing me with his excited eyes,
and perhaps perceived in my own an irrepressible

smile at his perplexity. "' Swing ahead, in Heaven's name,' you want to say, 'and much good may it do you.' I don't know whether you are laughing at my scruples or at what possibly strikes you as my depravity. I doubt," he went on gravely, "whether I have an inclination toward wrong-doing; if I have, I am sure I shall not prosper in it. I honestly believe I may safely take out a licence to amuse myself. But it isn't that I think of, any more than I dream of, playing with suffering. Pleasure and pain are empty words to me; what I long for is knowledge—some other knowledge than comes to us in formal, colour-less, impersonal precept. You would understand all this better if you could breathe for an hour the musty in-door atmosphere in which I have always lived. To break a window and let in light and air— I feel as if at last I must *act!*"

"Act, by all means, now and always, when you have a chance," I answered. "But don't take things too hard, now or ever. Your long confinement makes you think the world better worth knowing than you are likely to find it. A man with as good a head and heart as yours has a very ample world within himself, and I am no believer in art for art, nor in what's called

'life' for life's sake.   Nevertheless, take your plunge,
and come and tell me whether you have found the
pearl of wisdom."   He frowned a little, as if he
thought my sympathy a trifle meagre.   I shook him
by the hand and laughed.   "The pearl of wisdom,"
I cried, " is love ; honest love in the most convenient
concentration of experience !   I advise you to fall in
love."   He gave me no smile in response, but drew
from his pocket the letter of which I have spoken,
held it up, and shook it solemnly.   "What is it ?" I
asked.

" It is my sentence ! "

" Not of death, I hope ! "

" Of marriage."

" With whom ? "

" With a person I don't love."

This was serious.   I stopped smiling and begged
him to explain.

" It is the singular part of my story," he said at
last.   " It will remind you of an old-fashioned
romance.   Such as I sit here, talking in this wild
way, and tossing off provocations to destiny, my
destiny is settled and sealed.   I am engaged, I am
given in marriage.   It's a bequest of the past—the

past I had no hand in! The marriage was arranged
by my father, years ago, when I was a boy. The
young girl's father was his particular friend; he
was also a widower, and was bringing up his
daughter, on his side, in the same severe seclusion
in which I was spending my days. To this day I
am unacquainted with the origin of the bond of union
between our respective progenitors. Mr. Vernor was
largely engaged in business, and I imagine that once
upon a time he found himself in a financial strait and
was helped through it by my father's coming forward
with a heavy loan, on which, in his situation, he could
offer no security but his word. Of this my father
was quite capable. He was a man of dogmas, and
he was sure to have a rule of life—as clear as if it
had been written out in his beautiful copper plate
hand—adapted to the conduct of a gentleman toward
a friend in pecuniary embarrassment. What is more,
he was sure to adhere to it. Mr. Vernor, I believe,
got on his feet, paid his debt, and vowed my father
an eternal gratitude. His little daughter was the
apple of his eye, and he pledged himself to bring her
up to be the wife of his benefactor's son. So our fate
was fixed, parentally, and we have been educated for

each other. I have not seen my betrothed since she
was a very plain-faced little girl in a sticky pinafore,
hugging a one-armed doll—of the male sex, I believe
—as big as herself. Mr. Vernor is in what is called
the Eastern trade, and has been living these many
years at Smyrna. Isabel has grown up there in a
white-walled garden, in an orange grove, between her
father and her governess. She is a good deal my
junior; six months ago she was seventeen; when she
is eighteen we are to marry!"

He related all this calmly enough, without the
accent of complaint, dryly rather and doggedly, as if
he were weary of thinking of it. "It's a romance,
indeed, for these dull days," I said, "and I heartily
congratulate you. It's not every young man who
finds, on reaching the marrying age, a wife kept in
a box of rose-leaves for him. A thousand to one
Miss Vernor is charming; I wonder you don't post
off to Smyrna."

"You are joking," he answered, with a wounded
air, "and I am terribly serious. Let me tell you the
rest. I never suspected this superior conspiracy till
something less than a year ago. My father, wishing
to provide against his death, informed me of it very

solemnly. I was neither elated nor depressed; I received it, as I remember, with a sort of emotion which varied only in degree from that with which I could have hailed the announcement that he had ordered me a set of new shirts. I supposed that was the way that all marriages were made ; I had heard of their being made in heaven, and what was my father but a divinity? Novels and poems indeed talked about falling in love ; but novels and poems were one thing and life was another. A short time afterwards he introduced me to a photograph of my predestined, who has a pretty, but an extremely inanimate, face. After this his health failed rapidly. One night I was sitting, as I habitually sat for hours, in his dimly lighted room, near his bed, to which he had been confined for a week. He had not spoken for some time, and I supposed he was asleep ; but happening to look at him I saw his eyes wide open, and fixed on me strangely. He was smiling benignantly, intensely, and in a moment he beckoned to me. Then, on my going to him—' I feel that I shall not last long,' he said ; ' but I am willing to die when I think how comfortably I have arranged your future.' He was talking of death, and anything but grief at that

moment was doubtless impious and monstrous; but
there came into my heart for the first time a
throbbing sense of being over-governed. I said
nothing, and he thought my silence was all sorrow.
' I shall not live to see you married,' he went on,
' but since the foundation is laid, that little signifies;
it would be a selfish pleasure, and I have never
thought of myself but in you. To foresee your
future, in its main outline, to know to a certainty
that you will be safely domiciled here, with a wife
approved by my judgment, cultivating the moral
fruit of which I have sown the seed—this will content
me. But, my son, I wish to clear this bright vision
from the shadow of a doubt. I believe in your
docility; I believe I may trust the salutary force of
your respect for my memory. But I must remember
that when I am removed, you will stand here alone,
face to face with a hundred nameless temptations
to perversity. The fumes of unrighteous pride may
rise into your brain and tempt you, in the interest
of a vulgar theory which it will call your independence, to shatter the edifice I have so laboriously
constructed. So I must ask you for a promise—the
solemn promise you owe my condition.' And he

grasped my hand. 'You will follow the path I have marked ; you will be faithful to the young girl whom an influence as devoted as that which has governed your own young life has moulded into everything amiable ; you will marry Isabel Vernor.' This was pretty 'steep as we used to say at school. I was frightened ; I drew away my hand and asked to be trusted without any such terrible vow. My reluctance startled my father into a suspicion that the vulgar theory of independence had already been whispering to me. He sat up in his bed and looked at me with eyes which seemed to foresee a lifetime of odious ingratitude. . I felt the reproach ; I feel it now. I promised! And. even now I don't regret my promise nor complain of my father's tenacity. I feel, somehow, as if the seeds of ultimate repose had been sown in those unsuspecting years—as if after many days I might gather the mellow fruit. But after many days! I will keep my promise, I will obey ; but I want to *live* first!"

"My dear fellow, you are living now. All this passionate consciousness of your situation is a very ardent life. I wish I could say as much for my own."

"I want to forget my situation. I want to spend three months without thinking of the past or the future, grasping whatever the present offers me. Yesterday, I thought I was in a fair way to sail with the tide. But this morning comes this memento!" And he held up his letter again.

"What is it?"

"A letter from Smyrna."

"I see you have not yet broken the seal."

"No, nor do I mean to, for the present. It contains bad news."

"What do you call bad news?"

"News that I am expected in Smyrna in three weeks. News that Mr. Vernor disapproves of my roving about the world. News that his daughter is standing expectant at the altar."

"Is not this pure conjecture?"

"Conjecture, possibly, but safe conjecture. As soon as I looked at the letter, something smote me at the heart. Look at the device on the seal, and I am sure you will find it's *Tarry not!*" And he flung the letter on the grass.

"Upon my word, you had better open it," I said.

"If I were to open it and read my summons, do

you know what I should do? I should march home and ask the Oberkellner how one gets to Smyrna, pack my trunk, take my ticket, and not stop till I arrived. I know I should; it would be the fascination of habit. The only way, therefore, to wander to my rope's end is to leave the letter unread."

" In your place," I said, " curiosity would make me open it."

He shook his head. " I have no curiosity! For a long time now the idea of my marriage has ceased to be a novelty, and I have contemplated it mentally in every possible light. I fear nothing from that side, but I do fear something from conscience. I want my hands tied. Will you do me a favour? Pick up the letter, put it into your pocket, and keep it till I ask you for it. When I do, you may know that I am at my rope's end."

I took the letter, smiling. " And how long is your rope to be? The Homburg season doesn't last for ever."

" Does it last a month? Let that be my season! A month hence you will give it back to me."

" To-morrow, if you say so. Meanwhile, let it rest in peace!" And I consigned it to the most sacred

interstice of my pocket-book. To say that I was
disposed to humour the poor fellow would seem to be
saying that I thought his request fantastic. It was
his situation, by no fault of his own, that was fantastic, and he was only trying to be natural. He
watched me put away the letter, and when it had
disappeared gave a soft sigh of relief. The sigh was
natural, and yet it set me thinking. His general recoil
from an immediate responsibility imposed by others
might be wholesome enough ; but if there was an old
grievance on one side, was there not possibly a new-
born delusion on the other ? It would be unkind to
withhold a reflection that might serve as a warning ;
so I told him, abruptly, that I had been an undis-
covered spectator, the night before, of his exploits at
roulette.

He blushed deeply, but he met my eyes with the
same clear good-humour.

" Ah, then you saw that wonderful lady ? "

" Wonderful she was indeed. I saw her afterwards,
too, sitting on the terrace in the starlight. I imagine
she was not alone."

" No, indeed, I was with her—for nearly an hour.
Then I walked home with her."

"Ah! And did you go in?"

"No, she said it was too late to ask me; though she remarked that in a general way she did not stand upon ceremony."

"She did herself injustice. When it came to losing your money for you, she made you insist."

"Ah, you noticed that too?" cried Pickering, still quite unconfused. "I felt as if the whole table were staring at me; but her manner was so gracious and reassuring that I supposed she was doing nothing unusual. She confessed, however, afterwards, that she is very eccentric. The world began to call her so, she said, before she ever dreamed of it, and at last finding that she had the reputation, in spite of herself, she resolved to enjoy its privileges. Now, she does what she chooses."

"In other words, she is a lady with no reputation to lose!"

Pickering seemed puzzled; he smiled a little. "Is not that what you say of bad women?"

"Of some—of those who are found out."

"Well," he said, still smiling, "I have not yet found out Madame Blumenthal."

"If that's her name, I suppose she's German."

"Yes; but she speaks English so well that you wouldn't know it. She is very clever. Her husband is dead."

I laughed involuntarily at the conjunction of these facts, and Pickering's clear glance seemed to question my mirth. "You have been so bluntly frank with me," I said, "that I too must be frank. Tell me, if you can, whether this clever Madame Blumenthal, whose husband is dead, has given a point to your desire for a suspension of communication with Smyrna."

He seemed to ponder my question, unshrinkingly. "I think not," he said, at last. "I have had the desire for three months; I have known Madame Blumenthal for less than twenty-four hours."

"Very true. But when you found this letter of yours on your plate at breakfast, did you seem for a moment to see Madame Blumenthal sitting opposite?"

"Opposite?"

"Opposite, my dear fellow, or anywhere in the neighbourhood. In a word, does she interest you?"

"Very much!" he cried, joyously.

"Amen!" I answered, jumping up with a laugh. "And now, if we are to see the world in a month, there is no time to lose. Let us begin with the Hardtwald."

Pickering rose, and we strolled away into the forest, talking of lighter things. At last we reached the edge of the wood, sat down on a fallen log, and looked out across an interval of meadow at the long wooded waves of the Taunus. What my friend was thinking of, I can't say; I was meditating on his queer biography and letting my wonderment wander away to Smyrna. Suddenly I remembered that he possessed a portrait of the young girl who was waiting for him there in a white-walled garden. I asked him if he had it with him. He said nothing but gravely took out his pocket-book and drew forth a small photograph. It represented, as the poet says, a simple maiden in her flower—a slight young girl, with a certain childish roundness of contour. There was no ease in her posture; she was standing, stiffly and shyly, for her likeness; she wore a short-waisted white dress; her arms hung at her sides and her hands were clasped in front; her head was bent downward a little, and her dark eyes fixed. But her awkwardness was as pretty as that of some angular seraph in a mediæval carving, and in her timid gaze there seemed to lurk the questioning gleam of childhood. "What is this for?" her charming eyes appeared to ask; "why have I been dressed up for this ceremony in a white frock and amber beads?"

"Gracious powers!" I said to myself; "what an enchanting thing is innocence!"

"That portrait was taken a year and a half ago," said Pickering, as if with an effort to be perfectly just. "By this time, I suppose, she looks a little wiser."

"Not much, I hope," I said, as I gave it back. "She is very sweet!"

"Yes, poor girl, she is very sweet—no doubt!" And he put the thing away without looking at it.

We were silent for some moments. At last, abruptly—"My dear fellow," I said, "I should take some satisfaction in seeing you immediately leave Homburg."

"Immediately?"

"To-day—as soon as you can get ready."

He looked at me, surprised, and little by little he blushed. "There is something I have not told you," he said ; "something that your saying that Madame Blumenthal has no reputation to lose has made me half afraid to tell you."

"I think I can guess it. Madame Blumenthal has asked you to come and play her game for her again."

"Not at all!" cried Pickering, with a smile of triumph. "She says that she means to play no more for the present. She has asked me to come and take tea with her this evening."

"Ah, then," I said, very gravely, "of course you can't leave Homburg."

He answered nothing, but looked askance at me, as if he were expecting me to laugh. "Urge it strongly," he said in a moment. "Say it's my duty —that I *must.*"

I didn't quite understand him, but, feathering the shaft with a harmless expletive, I told him that unless he followed my advice I would never speak to him again.

He got up, stood before me, and struck the ground with his stick. "Good !" he cried, "I wanted an occasion to break a rule—to leap a barrier. Here it is! I stay!"

I made him a mock bow for his energy. "That's

very fine," I said ; "but now to put you in a proper
mood for Madame Blumenthal's tea, we will go and
listen to the band play Schubert under the lindens."
And we walked back through the woods.

I went to see Pickering the next day, at his inn,
and on knocking, as directed, at his door, was surprised to hear the sound of a loud voice within. My
knock remained unnoticed, so I presently introduced
myself. I found no company, but I discovered my
friend walking up and down the room and apparently
declaiming to himself from a little volume bound in
white vellum. He greeted me heartily, threw his
book on the table, and said that he was taking a
German lesson.

"And who is your teacher?" I asked, glancing
at the book.

He rather ,avoided meeting my eye, as he answered, after an instant's delay, "Madame Blumenthal."

"Indeed ! Has she written a grammar?"

"It's not a grammar ; it's a tragedy." And he
handed me the book.

I opened it, and beheld, in delicate type, with a
very large margin, an *Historisches Trauerspiel* in five

acts, entitled "Cleopatra." There were a great many marginal corrections and annotations, apparently from the author's hand; the speeches were very long, and there was an inordinate number of soliloquies by the heroine. One of them, I remember, towards the end of the play, began in this fashion—

"What, after all, is life but sensation, and sensation but deception?—reality that pales before the light of one's dreams, as Octavia's dull beauty fades beside mine? But let me believe in some intenser bliss and seek it in the arms of death!"

"It seems decidedly passionate," I said. "Has the tragedy ever been acted?"

"Never in public; but Madame Blumenthal tells me that she had it played at her own house in Berlin, and that she herself undertook the part of the heroine."

Pickering's unworldly life had not been of a sort to sharpen his perception of the ridiculous, but it seemed to me an unmistakable sign of his being under the charm, that this information was very soberly offered. He was preoccupied, he was irresponsive to my experimental observations on vulgar topics—the hot weather, the inn, the advent of

Adelina Patti. At last, uttering his thoughts, he announced that Madame Blumenthal had proved to be
an extraordinarily interesting woman. He seemed
to have quite forgotten our long talk in the Hardtwald, and betrayed no sense of this being a confession
that he had taken his plunge and was floating with
the current. He only remembered that I had spoken
slightingly of the lady, and he now hinted that it
behoved me to amend my opinion. I had received
the day before so strong an impression of a sort of
spiritual fastidiousness in my friend's nature, that
on hearing now the striking of a new hour, as it were,
in his consciousness, and observing how the echoes
of the past were immediately quenched in its music,
I said to myself that it had certainly taken a delicate
hand to wind up that fine machine. No doubt
Madame Blumenthal was a clever woman. It is a
good German custom, at Homburg to spend the
hour preceding dinner in listening to the orchestra
in the Kurgarten; Mozart and Beethoven, for or-
ganisms in which the interfusion of soul and sense is
peculiarly mysterious, are a vigorous stimulus to the
appetite. Pickering and I conformed, as we had
done the day before, to the fashion, and when we

were seated under the trees, he began to expatiate on his friend's merits.

"I don't know whether she is eccentric or not," he said; "to me every one seems eccentric, and it's not for me, yet a while, to measure people by my narrow precedents. I never saw a gaming-table in my life before, and supposed that a gambler was of necessity some dusky villain with an evil eye. In Germany, says Madame Blumenthal, people play at roulette as they play at billiards, and her own venerable mother originally taught her the rules of the game. It is a recognised source of subsistence for decent people with small means. But I confess Madame Blumenthal might do worse things than play at roulette, and yet make them harmonious and beautiful. I have never been in the habit of thinking positive beauty the most excellent thing in a woman. I have always said to myself that if my heart were ever to be captured it would be by a sort of general grace—a sweetness of motion and tone—on which one could count for soothing impressions, as one counts on a musical instrument that is perfectly in tune. Madame Blumenthal has it—this grace that soothes and satisfies; and it seems the more perfect that it keeps order and harmony in a character really passionately ardent and active. With her eager nature and her innumerable accomplishments, nothing would be easier than that she should seem restless and aggressive. You will know her, and I leave you to judge whether she does seem so ! She has every gift, and culture has done everything for each. What goes on in her mind, I of course can't say ; what reaches the observer—the admirer—is simply a sort of fragrant emanation of intelligence and sympathy."

" Madame Blumenthal," I said, smiling, " might be the loveliest woman in the world, and you the object of her choicest favours, and yet what I should most envy you would be, not your peerless friend, but your beautiful imagination."

" That's a ' polite way of calling me a fool," said Pickering. " You are a sceptic, a cynic, a satirist ! I hope I shall be a long time coming to that."

" You will make the journey fast if you travel by express trains. But pray tell me, have you ventured to intimate to Madame Blumenthal your high opinion of her ? "

"I don't know what I may have said. She listens
even better than she talks, and I think it possible
I may have made her listen to a great deal of non-
sense. For after the first few words I exchanged
with her I was conscious of an extraordinary evapo-
ration of all my old diffidence. I have, in truth, I
suppose," he added, in a moment, "owing to my
peculiar circumstances, a great accumulated fund of
unuttered things of all sorts to get rid of. Last
evening, sitting there before that charming woman,
they came swarming to my lips. Very likely I
poured them all out. I have a sense of having
enshrouded myself in a sort of mist of talk, and of
seeing her lovely eyes shining through it opposite to
me, like fog-lamps at sea." And here, if I remember
rightly, Pickering broke off into an ardent parenthesis,
and declared that Madame Blumenthal's eyes had
something in them that he had never seen in any others.
"It was a jumble of crudities, and inanities," he went
on ; "they must have seemed to her great rubbish ;
but I felt the wiser and the stronger, somehow, for
having fired off all my guns—they could hurt nobody now if they hit—and I imagine I might have
gone far without finding another woman in whom

such an exhibition would have provoked so little of mere cold amusement."

"Madame Blumenthal, on the contrary," I surmised, "entered into your situation with warmth."

"Exactly so—the greatest! She has felt and suffered, and now she understands!"

"She told you, I imagine, that she understood you as if she had made you, and she offered to be your guide, philosopher and friend."

"She spoke to me," Pickering answered, after a pause, "as I had never been spoken to before, and she offered me formally all the offices of a woman's friendship."

"Which you as formally accepted?"

"To you the scene sounds absurd, I suppose, but allow me to say I don't care!" Pickering spoke with an air of genial defiance which was the most inoffensive thing in the world. "I was very much moved; I was in fact, very much excited. I tried to say something, but I couldn't; I had had plenty to say before, but now I stammered and bungled, and at last I bolted out of the room."

"Meanwhile she had dropped her tragedy into your pocket!"

"Not at all. I had seen it on the table before she came in. Afterwards she kindly offered to read German aloud with me, for the accent, two or three times a week. 'What shall we begin with?' she asked. 'With this!' I said, and held up the book. And she let me take it to look it over."

I was neither a cynic nor a satirist, but even if I had been, I might have been disarmed by Pickering's assurance, before we parted, that Madame Blumenthal wished to know me and expected him to introduce me. Among the foolish things which, according to his own account, he had uttered, were some generous words in my praise, to which she had civilly replied. I confess I was curious to see her, but I begged that the introduction should not be immediate, for I wished to let Pickering work out his destiny alone. For some days I saw little of him, though we met at the Kursaal and strolled occasionally in the park. I watched, in spite of my desire to let him alone, for the signs and portents of the world's action upon him—of that portion of the world, in especial, of which Madame Blumenthal had constituted herself the agent. He seemed very happy, and gave me in a dozen ways an impression of increased

self-confidence and maturity. His mind was admirably active, and always, after a quarter of an hour's
talk with him, I asked myself what experience could
really do, that innocence had not done, to make it
bright and fine. I was struck with his deep enjoy-
ment of the whole spectacle of foreign life—its
novelty, its picturesqueness, its light and shade—and
with the infinite freedom with which he felt he could
go and come and rove and linger and observe it all.
It was an expansion, an awakening, a coming to moral
manhood. Each time I met him he spoke a little
less of Madame Blumenthal; but he let me know
generally that he saw her often, and continued to
admire her. I was forced to admit to myself, in spite
of preconceptions, that if she were really the ruling
star of this happy season, she must be a very superior
woman. Pickering had the air of an ingenuous young
philosopher sitting at the feet of an austere muse,
and not of a sentimental spendthrift dangling about
some supreme incarnation of levity.

II

MADAME BLUMENTHAL seemed, for the time, to have abjured the Kursaal, and I never caught a glimpse of her. Her young friend, apparently, was an interesting study, and the studious mind prefers seclusion.

She reappeared, however, at last, one evening at the opera, where from my chair I perceived her in a box, looking extremely pretty. Adelina Patti was singing, and after the rising of the curtain I was occupied with the stage; but on looking round when it fell for the *entr'acte*, I saw that the authoress of "Cleopatra" had been joined by her young admirer. He was sitting a little behind her, leaning forward, looking over her shoulder and listening, while she, slowly moving her fan to fro and letting her eye wander over the house, was apparently talking of this person and that. No doubt she was saying sharp

things ; but Pickering was not laughing; his eyes
were following her covert indications; his mouth
was half open, as it always was when he was interested ; he looked intensely serious. I was glad
that, having her back to him, she was unable to see
how he looked. It seemed the proper moment to
present myself and make her my bow; but just as
I was about to leave my place, a gentleman, whom
in a moment I perceived to be an old acquaintance, came to occupy the next chair. Recognition
and mutual greetings followed, and I was forced to
postpone my visit to Madame Blumenthal. I was
not sorry, for it very soon occurred to me that Niedermeyer would be just the man to give me a fair
prose version of Pickering's lyric tributes to his
friend. He was an Austrian by birth, and had
formerly lived about Europe a great deal in a series
of small diplomatic posts. England especially he
had often visited, and he spoke the language almost
without accent. I had once spent three rainy days with
him in the house of an English friend in the country.
He was a sharp observer and a good deal of a
gossip ; he knew a little something about every one,
and about some people everýthing. His knowledge

on social matters generally had the quality of all German science ; it was copious, minute, exhaustive.

"Do tell me," I said, as we stood looking round the house, "who and what is the lady in white, with the young man sitting behind her."

"Who ?" he answered, dropping his glass. "Madame Blumenthal ! What ? It would take long to say. Be introduced ; it's easily done ; you will find her charming. Then, after a week, you will tell me what she is."

"Perhaps I should not. My friend there has known her a week, and I don't think he is yet able to give a coherent account of her."

He raised his glass again, and after looking a while, "I am afraid your friend is a little—what do you call it ?—a little 'soft.' Poor fellow ! he's not the first. I have never known this lady that she has not had some eligible youth hovering about in some such attitude as that, undergoing the softening process. She looks wonderfully well, from here. It's extraordinary how those women last !"

"You don't mean, I take it, when you talk about 'those women,' that Madame Blumenthal is not embalmed, for duration, in a certain infusion of respectability?"

"Yes and no. The atmosphere that surrounds her is entirely of her own making. There is no reason in her antecedents that people should drop their voice when they speak of her. But some women are never at their ease till they have given some damnable twist or other to their position before the world. The attitude of upright virtue is unbecoming, like sitting too straight in a fauteuil. Don't ask me for opinions, however; content yourself with a few facts and with an anecdote. Madame Blumenthal is Prussian, and very well born. I remember her mother, an old Westphalian Gräfin, with principles marshalled out like Frederick the Great's grenadiers. She was poor, however, and her principles were an insufficient dowry for Anastasia, who was married very young to a vicious Jew, twice her own age. He was supposed to have money, but I am afraid he had less than was nominated in the bond, or else that his pretty young wife spent it very fast. She has been a widow these six or eight years, and has lived I imagine, in rather a hand-to-mouth fashion. I sup-

pose she is some six or eight-and-thirty years of
age. In winter one hears of her in Berlin, giving
little suppers to the artistic rabble there ; in summer
one often sees her across the green table at Ems
and Wiesbaden. She's very clever, and her cleverness has spoiled her. A year after her marriage she
published a novel, with her views on matrimony, in
the George Sand manner—beating the drum to
Madame Sand's trumpet. No doubt she was very
unhappy ; Blumenthal was an old beast. Since then
she has published a lot of literature—novels and
poems and pamphlets on every conceivable theme,
from the conversion of Lola Montez, to the Hegelian
philosophy. Her talk is much better than her
writing. Her *conjugophobia*—I can't call it by any
other name—made people think lightly of her at a
time when her rebellion against marriage was probably only theoretic. She had a taste for spinning
fine phrases, she drove her shuttle, and when she
came to the end of her yarn, she found that society
had turned its back. She tossed her head, declared
that at last she could breathe the sacred air of freedom, and formally announced that she had embraced
an 'intellectual' life. This meant unlimited *camara-*

derie with scribblers and daubers, Hegelian philosophers and Hungarian pianists. But she has been
admired also by a great many really clever men ;
there was a time, in fact, when she turned a head
as well set on its shoulders as this one!" And
Niedermeyer tapped his forehead. "She has a great
charm, and, literally, I know no harm of her. Yet
for all that, I am not going to speak to her; I am
not going near her box. I am going to leave her
to say, if she does me the honour to observe the
omission, that I too have gone over to the Philistines.
It's not that ; it is that there is something sinister
about the woman. I am too old for it to frighten
me, but I am good-natured enough for it to pain
me. Her quarrel with society has brought her no
happiness, and her outward charm is only the mask
of a dangerous discontent. Her imagination is
lodged where her heart should be! So long as
you amuse it, well and good ; she's radiant. But
the moment you let it flag, she is capable of
dropping you without a pang. If you land on your
feet, you are so much the wiser, simply ; but there
have been two or three, I believe, who have almost
broken their necks in the fall."

"You are reversing your promise," I said, "and giving me an opinion, but not an anecdote."

"This is my anecdote. A year ago a friend of mine made her aquaintance in Berlin, and though he was no longer a young man, and had never been what is called a susceptible one, he took a great fancy to Madame Blumenthal. He's a major in the Prussian artillery—grizzled, grave, a trifle severe, a man every way firm in the faith of his fathers. It's a proof of Anastasia's charm that such a man should have got into the habit of going to see her every day of his life. But the major was in love, or next door to it! Every day that he called he found her scribbling away at a little ormolu table on a lot of half-sheets of note-paper. She used to bid him sit down and hold his tongue for a quarter of an hour, till she had finished her chapter; she was writing a novel, and it was promised to a publisher. Clorinda, she confided to him, was the name of the injured heroine. The major, I imagine, had never read a work of fiction in his life, but he knew by hearsay that Madame Blumenthal's literature, when put forth in pink covers, was subversive of several respectable institutions. Besides, he didn't believe in women

knowing how to write at all, and it irritated him to
see this inky goddess correcting proof-sheets under
his nose—irritated him the more that, as I say, he
was in love with her and that he ventured to believe
she had a kindness for his years and his honours.
And yet she was not such a woman as he could
easily ask to marry him. The result of all this was
that he fell into the way of railing at her intellectual
pursuits and saying he should like to run his
sword through her pile of papers. A woman was
clever enough when she could guess her husband's
wishes, and learned enough when she could read
him the newspapers. At last, one day, Madame
Blumenthal flung down her pen and announced in
triumph that she had finished her novel. Clorinda
had expired in the arms of—some one else than her
husband. The major, by way of congratulating her,
declared that her novel was immoral rubbish, and
that her love of vicious paradoxes was only a peculiarly depraved form of coquetry. He added,
however, that he loved her in spite of her follies,
and that if she would formally abjure them he would
as formally offer her his hand. They say that women
like to be snubbed by military men. I don't know,

I'm sure ; I don't know how much pleasure, on this occasion, was mingled with Anastasia's wrath. But her wrath was very quiet, and the major assured me it made her look uncommonly pretty. 'I have told you before,' she says, 'that I write from an inner need. I write to unburden my heart, to satisfy my conscience. You call my poor efforts coquetry, vanity, the desire to produce a sensation. I can prove to you that it is the quiet labour itself I care for, and not the world's more or less flattering attention to it!' And seizing the history of Clorinda she thrust it into the fire. The major stands staring, and the first thing he knows she is sweeping him a great curtsey and bidding him farewell for ever. Left alone and recovering his wits, he fishes out Clorinda from the embers and then proceeds to thump vigorously at the lady's door. But it never opened, and from that day to the day three months ago when he told me the tale, he had not beheld her again."

" By Jove, it's a striking story," I said. " But the question is, what does it prove ? "

" Several things. First (what I was careful not to tell my friend), that Madame Blumenthal cared for him a trifle more than he supposed ; second, that he cares for her more than ever; third, that the performance was a master-stroke, and that her allowing him to force an interview upon her again is only a question of time."

"And last?" I asked.

"This is another anecdote. The other day, Unter den Linden, I saw on a bookseller's counter a little pink-covered romance—"Sophronia," by Madame Blumenthal. Glancing through it, I observed an extraordinary abuse of asterisks; every two or three pages the narrative was adorned with a portentous blank, crossed with a row of stars."

"Well, but poor Clorinda?" I objected, as Niedermeyer paused.

"Sophronia, my dear fellow, is simply Clorinda re-named by the baptism of fire. The fair author came back, of course, and found Clorinda tumbled upon the floor, a good deal scorched, but on the whole more frightened than hurt. She picks her up, brushes her off and sends her to the printer. Wherever the flames had burnt a hole, she swings a constellation! But if the major is prepared to drop a penitent tear over the ashes of Clorinda, I shall not whisper to him that the urn is empty."

Even Adelina Patti's singing, for the next half-hour, but half availed to divert me from my quickened curiosity to behold Madame Blumenthal face to face. As soon as the curtain had fallen again, I repaired to her box and was ushered in by Pickering with zealous hospitality. His glowing smile seemed to say to me "Ay, look for yourself, and adore!" Nothing could have been more gracious than the lady's greeting, and, I found, somewhat to my surprise, that her prettiness lost nothing on a nearer view. Her eyes indeed were the finest I have ever seen—the softest, the deepest, the most intensely responsive. In spite of something faded and jaded in her physiognomy, her movements, her smile, and the tone of her voice, especially when she laughed, had an almost girlish frankness and spontaneity. She looked at you very hard with her radiant gray eyes, and she indulged while she talked in a superabundance of restless, rather affected little gestures, as if to make you take her meaning in a certain very particular and superfine sense. I wondered whether after a while this might not fatigue one's attention; then meeting her charming eyes, I said, Not for a long time. She was very clever, and, as Pickering had said, she spoke English

admirably. I told her, as I took my seat beside
her, of the fine things I had heard about her from my
friend, and she listened, letting me go on some time,
and exaggerate a little, with her fine eyes fixed full
upon me. "Really?" she suddenly said, turning
short round upon Pickering, who stood behind us,
and looking at him in the same way. "Is that the
way you talk about me?"

He blushed to his eyes, and I repented. She suddenly began to laugh; it was then I observed how
sweet her voice was in laughter. We talked after
this of various matters, and in a little while I com-
plimented her on her excellent English, and asked
if she had learned it in England.

"Heaven forbid!" she cried. "I have never been
there and wish never to go. I should never get on
with the —" I wondered what she was going to say;
the fogs, the smoke, or whist with sixpenny stakes?
.—"I should never get on," she said, "with the aris-
tocracy! I am a fierce democrat—I am not ashamed
of it. I hold opinions which would make my
ancestors turn in their graves. I was born in the
lap of feudalism. I am a daughter of the crusaders.
But I am a revolutionist! I have a passion for free-

dom—my idea of happiness is to die on a great
barricade! It's to your great country I should like
to go. I should like to see the wonderful spectacle
of a great people free to do everything it chooses,
and yet never doing anything wrong!"

I replied, modestly, that, after all, both our freedom and our good conduct had their limits, and she
turned quickly about and shook her fan with a dramatic gesture at Pickering. "No matter, no matter!"
she cried, "I should like to see the country which
produced that wonderful young man. I think of it
as a sort of Arcadia—a land of the golden age. He's
so delightfully innocent! In this stupid old Germany, if a young man is innocent he's a fool; he
has no brains; he's not a bit interesting. But Mr.
Pickering says the freshest things, and after I have
laughed five minutes at their freshness it suddenly
occurs to me that they are very wise, and I think
them over for a week. True!" she went on, nodding
at him. "I call them inspired solecisms, and I treasure
them up. Remember that when I next laugh at you!"

Glancing at Pickering, I was prompted to believe
that he was in a state of beatific exaltation which
weighed Madame Blumenthal's smiles and frowns in

an equal balance. They were equally hers; they were links alike in the golden chain. He looked at me with eyes that seemed to say, "Did you ever hear such wit? Did you ever see such grace?" It seemed to me that he was but vaguely conscious of the meaning of her words; her gestures, her voice and glance, made an absorbing harmony. There is something painful in the spectacle of absolute enthralment, even to an excellent cause. I gave no response to Pickering's challenge, but made some remark upon the charm of Adelina Patti's singing. Madame Blumenthal, as became a "revolutionist," was obliged to confess that she could see no charm in it; it was meagre, it was trivial, it lacked soul. "You must know that in music, too," she said, "I think for myself!" And she began with a great many flourishes of her fan to explain what it was she thought. Remarkable things, doubtless; but I cannot answer for it, for in the midst of the explanation the curtain rose again. "You can't be a great artist without a great passion!" Madame Blumenthal was affirming. Before I had time to assent, Madame Patti's voice rose wheeling like a skylark, and rained down its silver notes. "Ah, give

me that art," I whispered, "and I will leave you your
passion!" And I departed for my own place in
the orchestra. I wondered afterwards whether the
speech had seemed rude, and inferred that it had
not, on receiving a friendly nod from the lady, in
the lobby, as the theatre was emptying itself. She
was on Pickering's arm, and he was taking her to
her carriage. Distances are short in Homburg, but
the night was rainy, and Madame Blumenthal ex-
hibited a very pretty satin-shod foot as a reason why,
though but a penniless widow, she should not walk
home. Pickering left us together a moment while
he went to hail the vehicle, and my companion
seized the opportunity, as she said, to beg me to
be so very kind as to come and see her. It was
for a particular reason! It was reason enough for
me, of course I answered, that she had given me
leave. She looked at me a moment with that extraordinary gaze of hers, which seemed so absolutely
audacious in its candour, and rejoined that I paid
more compliments than our young friend there, but
that she was sure I was not half so sincere. "But it's
about him I want to talk," she said. "I want to
ask you many things; I want you to tell me all

about him. He interests me; but you see my
sympathies are so intense, my imagination is so
lively, that I don't trust my own impressions. They
have misled me more than once!" And she gave
a little tragic shudder.

I promised to come and compare notes with her,
and we bade her farewell at her carriage door.
Pickering and I remained a while, walking up and
down the long glazed gallery of the Kursaal. I
had not taken many steps before I became aware
that I was beside a man in the very extremity of
love. "Isn't she wonderful?" he asked, with an
implicit confidence in my sympathy which it cost
me some ingenuity to elude. If he were really in
love, well and good! For although, now that I had
seen her, I stood ready to confess to large possibilities of fascination on Madame Blumenthal's part, and
even to certain possibilities of sincerity of which my
appreciation was vague, yet it seemed to me less omi-
nous that he should be simply smitten than that his
admiration should pique itself on being discriminating.
It was on his fundamental simplicity that I counted
for a happy termination of his experiment, and the
former of these alternatives seemed to me the

simpler. I resolved to hold my tongue and let him
run his course. He had a great deal to say about
his happiness, about the days passing like hours, the
hours like minutes, and about Madame Blumenthal
being a "revelation." "She was nothing to-night,"
he said; "nothing to what she sometimes is in the
way of brilliancy—in the way of repartee. If you
could only hear her when she tells her adventures!"

"Adventures?" I inquired. "Has she had adventures?"

"Of the most wonderful sort!" cried Pickering,
with rapture. "She hasn't vegetated, like me! She
has lived in the tumult of life. When I listen to
her reminiscences, it's like hearing the opening
tumult of one of Beethoven's symphonies, as it
loses itself in a triumphant harmony of beauty and
faith!"

I could only lift my eyebrows, but I desired to
know before we separated what he had done with
that troublesome conscience of his. "I suppose you
know, my dear fellow," I said, "that you are simply
in love. That's what they happen to call your state
of mind."

He replied with a brightening eye, as if he were

delighted to hear it—"So Madame Blumenthal told
me only this morning!" And seeing, I suppose,
that I was slightly puzzled, "I went to drive with
her," he continued ; "we drove to Königstein, to
see the old castle. We scrambled up into the heart
of the ruin and sat for an hour in one of the crum-
bling old courts. Something in the solemn stillness
of the place unloosed my tongue ; and while she sat
on an ivied stone, on the edge of the plunging wall,
I stood there and made a speech. She listened to
me, looking at me, breaking off little bits of stone
and letting them drop down into the valley. At
last she got up and nodded at me two or three times
silently, with a smile, as if she were applauding me
for a solo on the violin. 'You are in love,' she said.
'It's a perfect case!' And for some time she said
nothing more. But before we left the place she told
me that she owed me an answer to my speech. She
thanked me heartily, but she was afraid that if she
took me at my word she would be taking advantage
of my inexperience. I had known few women ; I
was too easily pleased ; I thought her better than
she really was. She had great faults ; I must know
her longer and find them out ; I must compare her

with other women—women younger, simpler, more
innocent, more ignorant; and then if I still did her
the honour to think well of her, she would listen to
me again. I told her that I was not afraid of pre-
ferring any woman in the world to her, and then she
repeated, ' Happy man, happy man ! you are in love,
you are in love ! '"

I called upon Madame Blumenthal a couple of
days later, in some agitation of thought. It has
been proved that there are, here and there, in the
world, such people as sincere impostors ; certain
characters who cultivate fictitious emotions in perfect
good faith. Even if this clever lady enjoyed poor
Pickering's bedazzlement, it was conceivable that,
taking vanity and charity together, she should care
more for his welfare than for her own entertainment ;
and her offer to abide by the result of hazardous
comparison with other women was a finer stroke
than her reputation had led me to expect. She received me in a shabby little sitting-room, littered
with uncut books and newspapers, many of which I
saw at a glance were French. One side of it was occupied by an open piano, surmounted by a jar full of
white roses. They perfumed the air ; they seemed to

me to exhale the pure aroma of Pickering's devotion.
Buried in an arm-chair, the object of this devotion
was reading the *Revue des Deux Mondes*. The purpose of my visit was not to admire Madame Blumenthal on my own account, but to ascertain how far I
might safely leave her to work her will upon my
friend. She had impugned my sincerity the evening
of the opera, and I was careful on this occasion to
abstain from compliments and not to place her on
her guard against my penetration. It is needless to
narrate our interview in detail; indeed, to tell the
perfect truth, I was punished for my rash attempt
to surprise her, by a temporary eclipse of my
own perspicacity. She sat there so questioning, so
perceptive, so genial, so generous, and so pretty withal,
that I was quite ready at the end of half an hour to
subscribe to the most comprehensive of Pickering's
rhapsodies. She was certainly a wonderful woman.
I have never liked to linger, in memory, on that half-
hour. The result of it was to prove that there were
many more things in the composition of a woman
who, as Niedermeyer said, had lodged her imagination in the place of her heart, than were dreamt of
in my philosophy. Yet, as I sat here stroking my

hat and balancing the account between nature and art in my affable hostess, I felt like a very competent philosopher. She had said she wished me to tell her everything about our friend, and she questioned me as to his family, his fortune, his antecedents and his character. All this was natural in a woman who had received a passionate declaration of love, and it was expressed with an air of charmed solicitude, a radiant confidence that there was really no mistake about his being a most distinguished young man, and that if I chose to be explicit, I might deepen her conviction to disinterested ecstasy, which might have almost provoked me to invent a good opinion, if I had not had one ready made. I told her that she really knew Pickering better than I did, and that until we met at Homburg I had not seen him since he was a boy.

"But he talks to you freely," she answered; "I know you are his confidant. He has told me certainly a great many things, but I always feel as if he were keeping something back; as if he were holding something behind him, and showing me only one hand at once. He seems often to be hovering on the edge of a secret. I have had several friendships in my life—thank Heaven! but I have had none more dear to me than this one. Yet in the midst of it I have the painful sense of my friend being half afraid of me; of his thinking me terrible, strange, perhaps a trifle out of my wits. Poor me! If he only knew what a plain good soul I am, and how I only want to know him and befriend him!"

These words were full of a plaintive magnanimity which made mistrust seem cruel. How much better I might play providence over Pickering's experiments with life, if I could engage the fine instincts of this charming woman on the providential side! Pickering's secret was, of course, his engagement to Miss Vernor; it was natural enough that he should have been unable to bring himself to talk of it to Madame Blumenthal. The simple sweetness of this young girl's face had not faded from my memory; I could not rid myself of the suspicion that in going further Pickering might fare much worse. Madame Blumenthal's professions seemed a virtual promise to agree with me, and after some hesitation I said that my friend had, in fact, a substantial secret, and that perhaps I

might do him a good turn by putting her in pos-
session of it. In as few words as possible I told her
that Pickering stood pledged by filial piety to marry
a young lady at Smyrna. She listened intently to
my story ; when I had finished it there was a faint
flush of excitement in each of her cheeks. She
broke out into a dozen exclamations of admiration
and compassion. " What a wonderful tale—what
a romantic situation ! No wonder poor Mr. Pickering
seemed restless and unsatisfied ; no wonder he wished
to put off the day of submission. And the poor
little girl at Smyrna, waiting there for the young
Western prince like the heroine of an Eastern tale !
She would give the world to see her photograph ;
did I think Mr. Pickering would show it to her ?
But never fear ; she would ask nothing indiscreet !
Yes, it was a marvellous story, and if she had invented it herself, people would have said it was
absurdly improbable." She left her seat and took
several turns about the room, smiling to herself and
uttering little German cries of wonderment. Suddenly she stopped before the piano and broke into
a little laugh ; the next moment she buried her
face in the great boquet of roses. It was time I

should go, but I was indisposed to leave her without obtaining some definite assurance that, as far as pity was concerned, she pitied the young girl at Smyrna more than the young man at Homburg.

"Of course you know what I wished in telling you this," I said, rising. "She is evidently a charming creature, and the best thing he can do is to marry her. I wished to interest you in that view of it."

She had taken one of the roses from the vase and was arranging it in the front of her dress. Suddenly, looking up, "Leave it to me, leave it to me!" she cried. "I am interested!" And with her little blue-gemmed hand she tapped her forehead. "I am deeply interested!"

And with this I had to content myself. But more than once, the next day, I repented of my zeal, and wondered whether a providence with a white rose in her bosom might not turn out a trifle too human. In the evening, at the Kursaal, I looked for Pickering, but he was not visible, and I reflected that my revelation had not as yet, at any rate, seemed to Madame Blumenthal a reason for prescribing a cooling-term to his passion. Very late, as I was turning away, I saw him arrive—with no small satisfaction, for I had determined to let him know immediately in what way I had attempted to serve him. But he straightway passed his arm through my own and led me off towards the gardens. I saw that he was too excited to allow me to speak first.

"I have burnt my ships!" he cried, when we were out of earshot of the crowd. "I have told her everything. I have insisted that it's simple torture for me to wait, with this idle view of loving her less. It's well enough for her to ask it, but I feel strong enough now to override her reluctance. I have cast off the millstone from round my neck. I care for nothing, I know nothing, but that I love her with every pulse of my being—and that everything else has been a hideous dream, from which she may wake me into blissful morning with a single word!"

I held him off at arm's-length and looked at him gravely. "You have told her, you mean, of your engagement to Miss Vernor?"

"The whole story! I have given it up—I have thrown it to the winds. I have broken utterly with the past. It may rise in its grave and give me its curse, but it can't frighten me now. I have a right to be happy, I have a right to be free, I have a right not to bury myself alive. It was not *I* who promised—I was not born then. I myself, my soul, my mind, my option—all this is but a month old! Ah," he went on, "if you knew the difference it makes—this having chosen and broken and spoken! I am twice the man I was yesterday! Yesterday I was afraid of her; there was a kind of mocking mystery of knowledge and cleverness about her, which oppressed me in the midst of my love. But now I am afraid of nothing but of being too happy!"

I stood silent, to let him spend his eloquence. But he paused a moment, and took off his hat and fanned himself. "Let me perfectly understand," I said at last. "You have asked Madame Blumenthal to be your wife?"

"The wife of my intelligent choice!"

"And does she consent?"

"She asks three days to decide."

"Call it four! She has known your secret since this morning. I am bound to let you know I told her."

"So much the better!" cried Pickering, without apparent resentment or surprise. "It's not a brilliant offer for such a woman, and in spite of what I have at stake I feel that it would be brutal to press her."

"What does she say to your breaking your promise?" I asked in a moment.

Pickering was too much in love for false shame. "She tells me that she loves me too much to find courage to condemn me. She agrees with me that I have a right to be happy. I ask no exemption from the common law. What I claim is simply freedom to try to be!"

Of course I was puzzled; it was not in that fashion that I had expected Madame Blumenthal to make use of my information. But the matter now was quite out of my hands, and all I could do was to bid my companion not work himself into a fever over either fortune.

The next day I had a visit from Niedermeyer, on whom, after our talk at the opera, I had left a card. We gossiped a while, and at last he said suddenly, "By the way, I have a sequel to the history of Clorinda. The major is at Homburg!"

"Indeed!" said I. "Since when?"

"These three days."

"And what is he doing?"

"He seems," said Niedermeyer with a laugh, "to be chiefly occupied in sending flowers to Madame Blumenthal. That is, I went with him the morning of his arrival to choose a nosegay, and nothing would suit him but a small haystack of white roses. I hope it was received."

"I can assure you it was," I cried. "I saw the lady fairly nestling her head in it. But I advise the major not to build upon that. He has a rival."

"Do you mean the soft young man of the other night?"

"Pickering is soft, if you will, but his softness seems to have served him. He has offered her everything, and she has not yet refused it." I had handed my visitor a cigar and he was puffing it in silence. At last he abruptly asked if I had been introduced to Madame Blumenthal, and, on my affirmative, inquired what I thought of her. "I will not tell you," I said, "or you'll call *me* soft."

He knocked away his ashes, eying me askance. "I have noticed your friend about," he said, "and

even if you had not told me, I should have known he
was in love. After he has left his adored, his face
wears for the rest of the day the expression with
which he has risen from her feet, and more than
once I have felt like touching his elbow, as you would
that of a man who has inadvertently come into a
drawing-room in his overshoes. You say he has
offered our friend everything ; but, my dear fellow,
he has not everything to offer her. He evidently is
as amiable as the morning, but the lady has no taste
for daylight."

"I assure you Pickering is a very interesting
fellow," I said.

"Ah, there it is ! Has he not some story or other ?
Isn't he an orphan, or a natural child, or consumptive,
or contingent heir to great estates ? She will read
his little story to the end, and close the book very
tenderly and smooth down the cover ; and then, when
he least expects it, she will toss it into the dusty
limbo of her other romances. She will let him
dangle, but she will let him drop !"

"Upon my word," I cried with heat, "if she does,
she will be a very unprincipled little creature !"

Niedermeyer shrugged his shoulders. " I never said she was a saint ! "

Shrewd as I felt Niedermeyer to be, I was not prepared to take his simple word for this event, and in the evening I received a communication which fortified my doubts. It was a note from Pickering, and it ran as follows—

" MY DEAR FRIEND,—I have every hope of being happy, but I am to go to Wiesbaden to learn my fate. Madame Blumenthal goes thither this afternoon to spend a few days, and she allows me to accompany her. Give me your good wishes ; you shall hear of the result. E.P."

One of the diversions of Homburg for new-comers is to dine in rotation at the different *tables d'hôte*. It so happened that, a couple of days later, Niedermeyer took pot-luck at my hotel, and secured a seat beside my own. As we took our places I found a letter on my plate, and, as it was postmarked Wiesbaden, I lost no time in opening it. It contained but three lines—

"I am happy—I am accepted—an hour ago. I can hardly believe it's your poor friend   E.P."

I placed the note before Niedermeyer; not exactly in triumph, but with the alacrity of all felicitous confutation. He looked at it much longer than was needful to read it, stroking down his beard gravely, and I felt it was not so easy to confute a pupil of the school of Metternich. At last, folding the note and handing it back, "Has your friend mentioned Madame Blumenthal's errand at Wiesbaden?" he asked.

"You look very wise. I give it up!" said I.

"She is gone there to make the major follow her. He went by the next train."

"And has the major, on his side, dropped you a line?"

"He is not a letter-writer."

"Well," said I, pocketing my letter, "with this document in my hand I am bound to reserve my judgment. We will have a bottle of Johannisberg, and drink to the triumph of virtue."

For a whole week more I heard nothing from Pickering—somewhat to my surprise, and, as the

days went by, not a little to my discomposure. I had
expected that his bliss would continue to overflow in
brief bulletins, and his silence was possibly an indi-
cation that it had been clouded. At last I wrote to
his hotel at Wiesbaden, but received no answer;
whereupon, as my next resource, I repaired to his
former lodging at Homburg, where I thought it
possible he had left property which he would sooner
or later send for. There I learned that he had
indeed just telegraphed from Cologne for his luggage.
To Cologne I immediately despatched a line of
inquiry as to his prosperity and the cause of his
silence. The next day I received three words in
answer—a simple uncommented request that I would
come to him. I lost no time, and reached him in the
course of a few hours. It was dark when I arrived,
and the city was sheeted in a cold autumnal rain.
Pickering had stumbled, with an indifference which
was itself a symptom of distress, on a certain
musty old Mainzerhof, and I found him sitting over
a smouldering fire in a vast dingy chamber which
looked as if it had grown gray with watching the
ennui of ten generations of travellers. Looking at
him, as he rose on my entrance, I saw that he was in

extreme tribulation. He was pale and haggard ; his
face was five years older. Now, at least, in all conscience, he had tasted of the cup of life! I was
anxious to know what had turned it so suddenly to
bitterness; but I spared him all importunate curiosity, and let him take his time. I accepted tacitly
his tacit confession of distress, and we made for a
while a feeble effort to discuss the picturesqueness
of Cologne. At last he rose and stood a long time
looking into the fire, while I slowly paced the length
of the dusky room.

"Well!" he said as I came back; "I wanted
knowledge, and I certainly know something I didn't
a month ago." And herewith, calmly and succinctly
enough, as if dismay had worn itself out, he related
the history of the foregoing days. He touched
lightly on details; he evidently never was to gush
as freely again as he had done during the prosperity
of his suit. He had been accepted one evening, as
explicitly as his imagination could desire, and had
gone forth in his rapture and roamed about till nearly
morning in the gardens of the Conversationhouse,
taking the stars and the perfumes of the summer
night into his confidence. "It is worth it all, almost,"

he said, "to have been wound up for an hour to that celestial pitch. No man, I am sure, can ever know it but once." The next morning he had repaired to Madame Blumenthal's lodging and had been met, to his amazement, by a naked refusal to see him. He had strode about for a couple of hours—in another mood—and then had returned to the charge. The servant handed him a three-cornered note; it contained these words: "Leave me alone to-day; I will give you ten minutes to-morrow evening." Of the next thirty-six hours he could give no coherent account, but at the appointed time Madame Blumenthal had received him. Almost before she spoke there had come to him a sense of the depth of his folly in supposing he knew her. "One has heard all one's days," he said, "of people removing the mask; it's one of the stock phrases of romance. Well, there she stood with her mask in her hand. Her face," he went on gravely, after a pause—"her face was horrible!" . . . . "I give you ten minutes," she had said, pointing to the clock. "Make your scene, tear your hair, brandish your dagger!" And she had sat down and folded her arms. "It's not a joke," she cried, "it's dead earnest; let us have it over.

You are dismissed—have you nothing to say?" He
had stammered some frantic demand for an explanation; and she had risen and come near him, looking
at him from head to feet, very pale, and evidently
more excited than she wished him to see. "I have
done with you!" she said with a smile; "you ought
to have done with me! It has all been delightful,
but there are excellent reasons why it should come
to an end." "You have been playing a part, then,"
he had gasped out; "you never cared for me?"
"Yes; till I knew you; till I saw how far you would
go. But now the story's finished; we have reached
the *dénoûment*. We will close the book and be
good friends." "To see how far I would go?" he
had repeated. "You led me on, meaning all the
while to do *this?*" "I led you on, if you will. I
received your visits, in season and out! Sometimes
they were very entertaining; sometimes they bored
me fearfully. But you were such a very curious case
of—what shall I call it?—of sincerity, that I determined to take good and bad together. I wanted
to make you commit yourself unmistakably. I
should have preferred not to bring you to this place;
but that too was necessary. Of course I can't marry

you ; I can do better. So can you, for that matter ;
thank your fate for it. You have thought wonders
of me for a month, but your good-humour wouldn't
last. I am too old and too wise ; you are too young
and too foolish. It seems to me that I have been
very good to you ; I have entertained you to the top
of your bent, and, except perhaps that I am a little
brusque just now, you have nothing to complain of.
I would have let you down more gently if I could
have taken another month to it ; but circumstances
have forced my hand. Abuse me, curse me, if you
like. I will make every allowance !" Pickering
listened to all this intently enough to perceive that,
as if by some sudden natural cataclysm, the ground
had broken away at his feet, and that he must recoil.
He turned away in dumb amazement. " I don't
know how I seemed to be taking it," he said, " but
she seemed really to desire—I don't know why—
something in the way of reproach and vituperation.
But I couldn't, in that way, have uttered a syllable.
I was sickened ; I wanted to get away into the air—
to shake her off and come to my senses. 'Have you
nothing, nothing, nothing to say ?' she cried, as if she
were disappointed, while I stood with my hand on

the door. 'Haven't I treated you to talk enough?'
I believe I answered. 'You will write to me then,
when you get home?' 'I think not,' said I. 'Six
months hence, I fancy, you will come and see me!'
'Never!' said I. 'That's a confession of stupidity,'
she answered. 'It means that, even on reflection,
you will never understand the philosophy of my
conduct.' The word 'philosophy' seemed so strange
that I verily believe I smiled. 'I have given you all
that you gave me,' she went on. 'Your passion was
an affair of the head.' 'I only wish you had told
me sooner that you considered it so!' I exclaimed.
And I went my way. The next day I came down
the Rhine. I sat all day on the boat, not knowing
where I was going, where to get off. I was in a kind
of ague of terror; it seemed to me I had seen something infernal. At last I saw the cathedral towers
here looming over the city. They seemed to
say something to me, and when the boat stopped,
I came ashore. I have been here a week. I have
not slept at night—and yet it has been a week
of rest!"

It seemed to me that he was in a fair way to
recover, and that his own philosophy, if left to take

its time, was adequate to the occasion. After his
story was once told I referred to his grievance but
once—that evening, later, as we were about to separate for the night. " Suffer me to say that there was
some truth in *her* account of your relations," I said.
" You were using her intellectually, and all the while,
without your knowing it, she was using you. It was
diamond cut diamond. Her needs were the more
superficial and she got tired of the game first." He
frowned and turned uneasily away, but without con-
tradicting me. I waited a few moments, to see if he
would remember, before we parted, that he had a
claim to make upon me. But he seemed to have
forgotten it.

The next day we strolled about the picturesque old
city, and of course, before long, went into the cathedral. Pickering said little ; he seemed intent upon
his own thoughts. He sat down beside a pillar near
a chapel, in front of a gorgeous window, and, leaving
him to his meditations, I wandered through the church.
When I came back I saw he had something to say;
But before he had spoken I laid my hand on his
shoulder and looked at him with a significant smile.
He slowly bent his head and dropped his eyes, with

a mixture of assent and humility. I drew forth from where it had lain untouched for a month the letter he had given me to keep, placed it silently on his knee, and left him to deal with it alone.

Half an hour later I returned to the same place, but he had gone, and one of the sacristans, hovering about and seeing me looking for Pickering, said he thought he had left the church. I found him in his gloomy chamber at the inn, pacing slowly up and down. I should doubtless have been at a loss to say just what effect I expected the letter from Smyrna to produce ; but his actual aspect surprised me. He was flushed, excited, a trifle irritated.

"Evidently," I said, "you have read your letter."

"It is proper I should tell you what is in it," he answered. "When I gave it to you a month ago, I did my friends injustice."

"You called it a 'summons,' I remember."

"I was a great fool ! It's a release !"

"From your engagement ?"

"From everything ! The letter, of course, is from Mr. Vernor. He desires to let me know at the earliest moment that his daughter, informed for the first time a week before of what had been expected

of her, positively refuses to be bound by the contract
or to assent to my being bound. She had been given
a week to reflect and had spent it in inconsolable
tears. She had resisted every form of persuasion;
from compulsion, writes Mr. Vernor, he naturally
shrinks. The young lady considers the arrangement
'horrible.' After accepting her duties cut and dried
all her life, she pretends at last to have a taste of her
own. I confess I am surprised; I had been given
to believe that she was stupidly submissive and
would remain so to the end of the chapter. Not a bit
of it. She has insisted on my being formally dismissed, and her father intimates that in case of non-
compliance she threatens him with an attack of brain-
fever. Mr. Vernor condoles with me handsomely,
and lets me know that the young lady's attitude
has been a great shock to his nerves. He adds that
he will not aggravate such regret as I may do him
the honour to entertain, by any allusions to his
daughter's charms and to the magnitude of my loss,
and he concludes with the hope that, for the comfort
of all concerned, I may already have amused my
fancy with other 'views.' He reminds me in a
postscript that, in spite of this painful occurrence,

the son of his most valued friend will always be a welcome visitor at his house. I am free, he observes; I have my life before me; he recommends an extensive course of travel. Should my wanderings lead me to the East, he hopes that no false embarrassment will deter me from presenting myself at Smyrna. He can promise me at least a friendly reception. It's a very polite letter."

Polite as the letter was, Pickering seemed to find no great exhilaration in having this famous burden so handsomely lifted from his spirit. He began to brood over his liberation in a manner which you might have deemed proper to a renewed sense of bondage. "Bad news," he had called his letter originally; and yet, now that its contents proved to be in flat contradiction to his foreboding, there was no impulsive voice to reverse the formula and declare the news was good. The wings of impulse in the poor fellow had of late been terribly clipped. It was an obvious reflection, of course, that if he had not been so stiffly certain of the matter a month before, and had gone through the form of breaking Mr. Vernor's seal, he might have escaped the purgatory of Madame Blumenthal's sub-acid blandish-

ments. But I left him to moralise in private; I
had no desire, as the phrase is, to rub it in. My
thoughts, moreover, were following another train ; I
was saying to myself that if to those gentle graces
of which her young visage had offered to my fancy
the blooming promise, Miss Vernor added in this
striking measure the capacity for magnanimous
action, the amendment to my friend's career had
been less happy than the rough draught. Presently,
turning about, I saw him looking at the young
lady's photograph. "Of course, now," he said, "I
have no right to keep it!" And before I could
ask for another glimpse of it, he had thrust it into
the fire.

"I am sorry to be saying it just now," I observed
after a while, "but I shouldn't wonder if Miss Vernor
were a charming creature."

"Go and find out," he answered gloomily. "The
coast is clear. My part is to forget her," he presently
added. "It ought not to be hard. But don't you
think," he went on suddenly, "that for a poor fellow who asked nothing of fortune but leave to sit
down in a quiet corner, it has been rather a cruel
pushing about ? "

Cruel indeed, I declared, and he certainly had the right to demand a clean page on the book of fate, and a fresh start. Mr. Vernor's advice was sound; he should amuse himself with a long journey. If it would be any comfort to him, I would go with him on his way. Pickering assented without enthusiasm; he had the embarrassed look of a man who, having gone to some cost to make a good appearance in a drawing-room, should find the door suddenly slammed in his face. We started on our journey, however, and little by little his enthusiasm returned. He was too capable of enjoying fine things to remain permanently irresponsive, and after a fortnight spent among pictures and monuments and antiquities, I felt that I was seeing him for the first time in his best and healthiest mood. He had had a fever and then he had had a chill; the pendulum had swung right and left in a manner rather trying to the machine; but now, at last, it was working back to an even, natural beat. He recovered in a measure the generous eloquence with which he had fanned his flame at Homburg, and talked about things with something of the same passionate freshness. One day when I was laid up at the inn at Bruges with a

lame foot, he came home and treated me to a
rhapsody about a certain meek-faced virgin of
Hans Memling, which seemed to me sounder sense
than his compliments to Madame Blumenthal. He
had his dull days and his sombre moods—hours of
irresistible retrospect ; but I let them come and go
without remonstrance, because I fancied they always
left him a trifle more alert and resolute. One evening
however, he sat hanging his head in so doleful a
fashion that I took the bull by the horns and told
him he had by this time surely paid his debt to
penitence, and that he owed it to himself to banish
that woman for ever from his thoughts.

He looked up, staring ; and then with a deep blush
—" That woman ? " he said. " I was not thinking of
Madame Blumenthal ! "

After this I gave another construction to his melancholy. Taking him with his hopes and fears, at the
end of six weeks of active observation and keen
sensation, Pickering was as fine a fellow as need be.
We made our way down to Italy and spent a fortnight at Venice. There something happened which
I had been confidently expecting ; I had said to myself that it was merely a question of time. We had

passed the day at Torcello, and came floating back in the glow of the sunset, with measured oar-strokes. " I am well on the way," Pickering said ; " I think I will go ! "

We had not spoken for an hour, and I naturally asked him, Where ? His answer was delayed by our getting into the Piazzetta. I stepped ashore first and then turned to help him. As he took my hand, he met my eyes, consciously, and it came. " To Smyrna ! "

A couple of days later he started. I had risked the conjecture that Miss Vernor was a charming creature, and six months afterwards he wrote me that I was right.

THE DIARY OF A MAN OF FIFTY.

FLORENCE, *April 5th,* 1874.—They told me I should find Italy greatly changed; and in seven and twenty years there is room for changes. But to me everything is so perfectly the same that I seem to be living my youth over again; all the forgotten impressions of that enchanting time come back to me. At the moment they were powerful enough; but they afterwards faded away. What in the world became of them? What ever becomes of such things, in the long intervals of consciousness? Where do they hide themselves away? in what unvisited cupboards and crannies of our being do they preserve themselves? They are like the lines of a letter written in sympathetic ink; hold the letter to the fire for a while and the grateful warmth brings out the invisible words. It is the warmth of this yellow sun of Florence that has been restoring the text of my own young romance; the thing has been lying before me to-day as a clear, fresh page. There have been moments during the last ten years when I have felt so portentously old, so fagged and finished, that I should have taken as a very bad joke any intimation that this present sense of juvenility was still in store for me. It won't last, at any rate; so I had better make the best of it. But I confess it surprises me. I have led too serious a life; but that perhaps, after all, preserves one's youth. At all events, I have travelled too far, I have worked too hard, I have lived in brutal climates and associated with tiresome people. When a man has reached his fifty-second year without being, materially, the worse for wear—when he has fair health, a fair fortune, a tidy conscience and a complete exemption from embarrassing relatives—I suppose he is bound, in delicacy, to write himself happy. But I confess I shirk this obligation. I have not been miserable; I won't go so far as to say that—or at least as to write it. But happiness—positive happiness—would have been something different. I don't know that it would have been better, by all measurements—that it would have left me better

off at the present time.   But it certainly would have
made this difference—that I should not have been
reduced, in pursuit of pleasant images, to disinter a
buried episode of more than a quarter of a century
ago.   I should have found entertainment more—
what shall I call it?—more contemporaneous.   I
should have had a wife and children, and I should
not be in the way of making, as the French say,
infidelities to the present.   Of course it's a great
gain to have had an escape, not to have committed
an act of thumping folly; and I suppose that, whatever serious step one might have taken at twenty-
five, after a struggle, and with a violent effort, and
however one's conduct might appear to be justified
by events, there would always remain a certain
element of regret; a certain sense of loss lurking
in the sense of gain ; a tendency to wonder, rather
wishfully, what *might* have been.   What might have
been, in this case, would, without doubt, have been
very sad, and what has been has been very cheerful
and comfortable; but there are nevertheless two or
three questions I might ask myself.   Why, for in-
stance, have I never married—why have I never been
able to care for any woman as I cared for that one ?

Ah, why are the mountains blue and why is the sunshine warm? Happiness mitigated by impertinent conjectures—that's about my ticket.

6th.—I knew it wouldn't last; it's already passing away. But I have spent a delightful day; I have been strolling all over the place. Everything reminds me of something else, and yet of itself at the same time; my imagination makes a great circuit and comes back to the starting-point. There is that well-remembered odour of spring in the air, and the flowers, as they used to be, are gathered into great sheaves and stacks, all along the rugged base of the Strozzi Palace. I wandered for an hour in the Boboli Gardens; we went there several times together. I remember all those days individually; they seem to me as yesterday. I found the corner where she always chose to sit— the bench of sun-warmed marble, in front of the screen of ilex, with that exuberant statue of Pomona just beside it. The place is exactly the same, except that poor Pomona has lost one of her tapering fingers. I sat there for half-an-hour, and it was strange how near to me she seemed. The place was perfectly empty—that is, it was filled with *her*. I closed my eyes and listened; I could almost hear the rustle of her dress on the gravel. Why do we make such an ado about death? What is it after all but a sort of refinement of life? She died ten years ago, and yet, as I sat there in the sunny stillness, she was a palpable, audible presence. I went afterwards into the gallery of the palace, and wandered for an hour from room to room. The same great pictures hung in the same places and the same dark frescoes arched above them. Twice, of old, I went there with her; she had a great understanding of art. She understood all sorts of things. Before the Madonna of the Chair I stood a long time. The face is not a particle like hers, and yet it reminded me of her. But everything does that. We stood and looked at it together once for half-an-hour; I remember perfectly what she said.

8*th.*—Yesterday I felt blue—blue and bored; and when I got up this morning I had half a mind to leave Florence. But I went out into the street, beside the Arno, and looked up and down—looked at the yellow river and the violet hills, and then decided to remain—or rather, I decided nothing.

I simply stood gazing at the beauty of Florence, and before I had gazed my fill I was in good-humour again, and it was too late to start for Rome. I strolled along the quay, where something presently happened that rewarded me for staying. I stopped in front of a little jeweller's shop, where a great many objects in mosaic were exposed in the window; I stood there for some minutes—I don't know why, for I have no taste for mosaic. In a moment a little girl came and stood beside me—a little girl with a frowsy Italian head, carrying a basket. I turned away, but, as I turned, my eyes happened to fall on her basket. It was covered with a napkin, and on the napkin was pinned a piece of paper, inscribed with an address. This address caught my glance—there was a name on it I knew. It was very legibly written—evidently by a scribe who had made up in zeal what was lacking in skill. *Contessa Salvi-Scarabelli, Via Ghibellina*—so ran the superscription; I looked at it for some moments; it caused me a sudden emotion. Presently the little girl, becoming aware of my attention, glanced up at me, wondering, with a pair of timid brown eyes.

"Are you carrying your basket to the Countess Salvi?" I asked.

The child stared at me. "To the Countess Scarabelli."

"Do you know the Countess?"

"Know her?" murmured the child, with an air of small dismay.

"I mean, have you seen her?"

"Yes, I have seen her." And then, in a moment, with a sudden soft smile—"*E bella!*" said the little girl. She was beautiful herself as she said it.

"Precisely; and is she fair or dark?"

The child kept gazing at me. "*Bionda—bionda*," she answered, looking about into the golden sunshine for a comparison.

"And is she young?"

"She is not young—like me. But she is not old like—like—"

"Like me, eh? And is she married?"

The little girl began to look wise. "I have never seen the Signor Conte."

"And she lives in Via Ghibellina?"

"*Sicuro.* In a beautiful palace."

I had one more question to ask, and I pointed

it with certain copper coins. " Tell me a little—
is she good ? "

The child inspected a moment the contents of her
little brown fist. "It's you who are good," she
answered.

" Ah, but the Countess?" I repeated.

My informant lowered her big brown eyes, with
an air of conscientious meditation that was in-
expressibly quaint. "To me she appears so," she
said at last, looking up.

" Ah, then she must be so," I said, " because, for
your age, you are very intelligent." And having
delivered myself of this compliment I walked away
and left the little girl counting her *soldi.*

I walked back to the hotel, wondering how I
could learn something about the Contessa Salvi-
Scarabelli. In the doorway I found the innkeeper,
and near him stood a young man whom I immediately perceived to be a compatriot and with
whom, apparently, he had been in conversation.

" I wonder whether you can give me a piece of
information," I said to the landlord. " Do you know
anything about the Count Salvi-Scarabelli ? "

The landlord looked down at his boots, then slowly

raised his shoulders, with a melancholy smile. " I have many regrets, dear sir——"

" You don't know the name ? "

" I know the name, assuredly. But I don't know the gentleman."

I saw that my question had attracted the attention of the young Englishman, who looked at me with a good deal of earnestness. He was apparently satisfied with what he saw, for he presently decided to speak.

" The Count Scarabelli is dead," he said, very gravely.

I looked at him a moment; he was a pleasing young fellow, " And his widow lives," I observed, " in Via Ghibellina ? "

" I daresay that is the name of the street." He was a handsome young Englishman, but he was also an awkward one; he wondered who I was and what I wanted, and he did me the honour to perceive that, as regards these points, my appearance was reassuring. But he hesitated, very properly, to talk with a perfect stranger about a lady whom he knew, and he had not the art to conceal his hesitation. I instantly felt it to be singular that though he regarded me as a perfect stranger, I had not the same feeling about him. Whether it was that I had seen him before, or simply that I was struck with his agreeable young face—at any rate, I felt myself as they say here, in sympathy with him. If I have seen him before I don't remember the occasion, and neither, apparently, does he ; I suppose it's only a part of the feeling I have had the last three days about everything. It was this feeling that made me suddenly act as if I had known him a long time.

" Do you know the Countess Salvi ? " I asked.

He looked at me a little, and then, without resenting the freedom of my question—" The Countess Scarabelli you mean," he said.

" Yes," I answered ; " she's the daughter."

" The daughter is a little girl."

" She must be grown up now. She must be—let me see—close upon thirty."

My young Englishman began to smile. "Of whom are you speaking ? "

" I was speaking of the daughter," I said, understanding his smile. " But I was thinking of the mother."

"Of the mother?"

"Of a person I knew twenty-seven years ago—
the most charming woman I have ever known. She
was the Countess Salvi—she lived in a wonderful
old house in Via Ghibellina."

"A wonderful old house!" my young Englishman
repeated.

"She had a little girl," I went on; "and the little
girl was very fair, like her mother; and the mother
and daughter had the same name—Bianca."   I
stopped and looked at my companion, and he
blushed a little. "And Bianca Salvi," I continued,
"was the most charming woman in the world."   He
blushed a little more, and I laid my hand on his
shoulder. "Do you know why I tell you this?
Because you remind me of what I was when I knew
her—when I loved her."   My poor young Englishman gazed at me with a sort of embarrassed and
fascinated stare, and still I went on. "I say that's
the reason I told you this—but you'll think it a
strange reason. You remind me of my younger
self. You needn't resent that—I was a charming
young fellow. The Countess Salvi thought so. Her
daughter thinks the same of you."

Instantly, instinctively he raised his hand to my arm. "Truly?"

"Ah, you are wonderfully like me!" I said, laughing. "That was just my state of mind. I wanted tremendously to please her." He dropped his hand and looked away, smiling, but with an air of ingenuous confusion which quickened my interest in him. "You don't know what to make of me," I pursued. "You don't know why a stranger should suddenly address you in this way and pretend to read your thoughts. Doubtless you think me a little cracked. Perhaps I am eccentric; but it's not so bad as that. I have lived about the world a great deal, following my profession, which is that of a soldier. I have been in India, in Africa, in Canada, and I have lived a good deal alone. That inclines people, I think, to sudden bursts of confidence. A week ago I came into Italy, where I spent six months when I was your age. I came straight to Florence—I was eager to see it again, on account of associations. They have been crowding upon me ever so thickly. I have taken the liberty of giving you a hint of them." The young man inclined himself a little, in silence, as if he had

been struck with a sudden respect. He stood and
looked away for a moment at the river and the
mountains. "It's very beautiful," I said.

"Oh, it's enchanting," he murmured.

"That's the way I used to talk. But that's
nothing to you."

He glanced at me again. "On the contrary, I
like to hear."

"Well, then, let us take a walk. If you too are
staying at this inn, we are fellow-travellers. We will
walk down the Arno to the Cascine. There are
several things I should like to ask of you."

My young Englishman assented with an air of
almost filial confidence, and we strolled for an hour
beside the river and through the shady alleys of that
lovely wilderness. We had a great deal of talk:
it's not only myself, it's my whole situation over
again.

"Are you very fond of Italy?" I asked.

He hesitated a moment. "One can't express
that."

"Just so; I couldn't express it. I used to try—
I used to write verses. On the subject of Italy I
was very ridiculous."

"So am I ridiculous," said my companion.

"No, my dear boy," I answered, "we are not ridiculous; we are two very reasonable, superior people."

"The first time one comes—as I have done—it's a revelation."

"Oh, I remember well; one never forgets it. It's an introduction to beauty."

"And it must be a great pleasure," said my young friend, "to come back."

"Yes, fortunately the beauty is always here. What form of it," I asked, "do you prefer?"

My companion looked a little mystified; and at last he said, "I am very fond of the pictures."

"So was I. And among the pictures, which do you like best?"

"Oh, a great many."

"So did I; but I had certain favourites."

Again the young man hesitated a little, and then he confessed that the group of painters he preferred on the whole to all others was that of the early Florentines.

I was was so struck with this that I stopped short. "That was exactly my taste!" And then I passed my hand into his arm and we went our way again.

We sat down on an old stone bench in the Cascine, and a solemn blank-eyed Hermes, with wrinkles accentuated by the dust of ages, stood above us and listened to our talk.

" The Countess Salvi died ten years ago," I said.

My companion admitted that he had heard her daughter say so.

" After I knew her she married again," I added. " The Count Salvi died before I knew her—a couple of years after their marriage."

" Yes, I have heard that."

" And what else have you heard ? "

My companion stared at me; he had evidently heard nothing.

" She was a very interesting woman—there are a great many things to be said about her. Later, perhaps, I will tell you. Has the daughter the same charm ? "

" You forget," said my young man, smiling, " that I have never seen the mother."

" Very true. I keep confounding. But the daughter—how long have you known her ? "

" Only since I have been here.   A very short
time."

" A week ? "

For a moment he said nothing.   " A month."

" That's just the answer I should have made.   A
week, a month—it was all the same to me."

" I think it is more than a month," said the young
man.

" It's probably six.   How did you make her
acquaintance ? "

" By a letter—an introduction given me by a friend
in England."

" The analogy is complete," I said.   " But the
friend who gave me my letter to Madame de Salvi
died many years ago.   He, too, admired her greatly.
I don't know why it never came into my mind that
her daughter might be living in Florence.   Somehow
I took for granted it was all over.   I never thought
of the little girl ; I never heard what had become of
her.   I walked past the palace yesterday and saw
that it was occupied ; but I took for granted it had
changed hands."

"The Countess Scarabelli," said my friend, "brought
it to her husband as her marriage-portion."

" I hope he appreciated it ! There is a fountain in the court, and there is a charming old garden beyond it. The Countess's sitting-room looks into that garden. The staircase is of white marble, and there is a medallion by Luca della Robbia set into the wall at the place where it makes a bend. Before you come into the drawing-room you stand a moment in a great vaulted place hung round with faded tapestry, paved with bare tiles, and furnished only with three chairs. In the drawing-room, above the fire-place, is a superb Andrea del Sarto. The furniture is covered with pale sea-green."

My companion listened to all this.

" The Andrea del Sarto is there ; it's magnificent. But the furniture is in pale red."

" Ah, they have changed it then—in twenty-seven years."

" And there's a portrait of Madame de Salvi," continued my friend.

I was silent a moment. " I should like to see that."

He too was silent. Then he asked, " Why don't you go and see it ? If you knew the mother so well, why don't you call upon the daughter ? "

" From what you tell me I am afraid."

" What have I told you to make you afraid ? "

I looked a little at his ingenuous countenance.
" The mother was a very dangerous woman."

The young Englishman began to blush again.
" The daughter is not," he said.

" Are you very sure ? "

He didn't say he was sure, but he presently
inquired in what way the Countess Salvi had been
dangerous.

" You must not ask me that," I answered ; " for,
after all, I desire to remember only what was good in
her." And as we walked back I begged him to render
me the service of mentioning my name to his friend,
and of saying that I had known her mother well and
that I asked permission to come and see her.

9th.—I have seen that poor boy half-a-dozen times
again, and a most amiable young fellow he is. He
continues to represent to me, in the most extraordinary manner, my own young identity ; the correspondence is perfect at all points, save that he is a
better boy than I. He is evidently acutely interested
in his Countess, and leads quite the same life with her
that I led with Madame de Salvi. He goes to see
her every evening and stays half the night ; these

Florentines keep the most extraordinary hours.   I remember, towards 3 A.M., Madame de Salvi used to turn me out.   " Come, come," she would say, "it's time to go.   If you were to stay later people might talk."   I don't know at what time he comes home, but I suppose his evening seems as short as mine did. To-day he brought me a message from his Contessa —a very gracious little speech.   She remembered often to have heard her mother speak of me—she called me her English friend.   All her mother's friends were dear to her, and she begged I would do her the honour to come and see her.   She is always at home of an evening.   Poor young Stanmer (he is of the Devonshire Stanmers—a great property) reported this speech verbatim, and of course it can't in the least signify to him that a poor grizzled, battered soldier, old enough to be his father, should come to call upon his *inammorata*.   But I remember how it used to matter to me when other men came ; that's a point of difference.   However, it's only because I'm so old.   At twenty-five I shouldn't have been afraid of myself at fifty-two.   Camerino was thirty-four—and then the others !   She was always at home in the evening, and they all used to come.

They were old Florentine names. But she used to let me stay after them all; she thought an old English name as good. What a transcendent co-quette! . . . But *basta così*, as she used to say. I meant to go to-night to Casa Salvi, but I couldn't bring myself to the point. I don't know what I'm afraid of; I used to be in a hurry enough to go there once. I suppose I am afraid of the very look of the place—of the old rooms, the old walls. I shall go to-morrow night. I am afraid of the very echoes.

10*th*.—She has the most extraordinary resemblance to her mother. When I went in I was tremendously startled; I stood staring at her. I have just come home; it is past midnight; I have been all the evening at Casa Salvi. It is very warm—my window is open—I can look out on the river, gliding past in the starlight. So, of old, when I came home, I used to stand and look out. There are the same cypresses on the opposite hills.

Poor young Stanmer was there, and three or four other admirers; they all got up when I came in. I think I had been talked about, and there was some curiosity. But why should I have been talked about? They were all youngish men—none of them of my time.

She is a wonderful likeness of her mother; I couldn't get over it. Beautiful like her mother, and yet with the same faults in her face; but with her mother's perfect head and brow and sympathetic, almost pitying, eyes. Her face has just that peculiarity of her mother's, which, of all human countenances that I have ever known, was the one that passed most quickly and completely from the expression of gaiety to that of repose. Repose, in her face, always suggested sadness; and while you were watching it with a kind of awe, and wondering of what tragic secret it was the token, it kindled, on the instant, into a radiant Italian smile. The Countess Scarabelli's smiles to-night, however, were almost uninterrupted. She greeted me—divinely, as her mother used to do; and young Stanmer sat in the corner of the sofa—as I used to do—and watched her while she talked. She is thin and very fair, and was dressed in light, vaporous black : that completes the resemblance. The house, the rooms, are almost absolutely the same ; there may be changes of detail, but they don't modify the general effect. There are the same precious pictures on the walls of the salon—the same great dusky fresco in the concave ceiling. The daughter is not rich, I suppose, any more than the mother. The furniture is worn and faded, and I was admitted by a solitary servant who carried a twinkling taper before me up the great dark marble staircase.

"I have often heard of you," said the Countess, as I sat down near her; "my mother often spoke of you."

"Often?" I answered. "I am surprised at that."

"Why are you surprised? Were you not good friends?"

"Yes, for a certain time—very good friends. But I was sure she had forgotten me."

"She never forgot," said the Countess, looking at me intently and smiling. "She was not like that."

"She was not like most other women in any way," I declared.

"Ah, she was charming," cried the Countess, rattling open her fan. "I have always been very curious to see you. I have received an impression of you."

"A good one, I hope."

She looked at me, laughing, and not answering this: it was just her mother's trick.

" ' My Englishman,' she used to call you—' *il mio Inglese.*' "

" I hope she spoke of me kindly," I insisted.

The Countess, still laughing, gave a little shrug, balancing her hand to and fro. " So-so ; I always supposed you had had a quarrel. You don't mind my being frank like this—eh ? "

" I delight in it ; it reminds me of your mother."

" Every one tells me that. But I am not clever like her. You will see for yourself."

" That speech," I said, " completes the resemblance. She was always pretending she was not clever, and in reality——"

" In reality she was an angel, eh ? To escape from dangerous comparisons I will admit then that I am clever. That will make a difference. But let us talk of you. You are very—how shall I say it ?— very eccentric."

" Is that what your mother told you ? "

" To tell the truth, she spoke of you as a great original. But aren't all Englishmen eccentric ? All except that one ! " and the Countess pointed to poor Stanmer, in his corner of the sofa.

"Oh, I know just what he is," I said.

"He's as quiet as a lamb—he's like all the world," cried the Countess.

"Like all the world—yes. He is in love with you."

She looked at me with sudden gravity. "I don't object to your saying that for all the world—but I do for him."

"Well," I went on, "he is peculiar in this: he is rather afraid of you."

Instantly she began to smile ; she turned her face toward Stanmer. He had seen that we were talking about him ; he coloured and got up—then came toward us.

"I like men who are afraid of nothing," said our hostess.

"I know what you want," I said to Stanmer. "You want to know what the Signora Contessa says about you.

Stanmer looked straight into her face, very gravely. "I don't care a straw what she says."

"You are almost a match for the Signora Contessa," I answered. "She declares she doesn't care a' pin's head what you think."

"I recognise the Countess's style!" Stanmer exclaimed, turning away.

"One would think," said the Countess, "that you were trying to make a quarrel between us."

I watched him move away to another part of the great saloon; he stood in front of the Andrea del Sarto, looking up at it. But he was not seeing it; he was listening to what we might say. I often stood there in just that way. "He can't quarrel with you, any more than I could have quarrelled with your mother."

"Ah, but you did. Something painful passed between you."

"Yes, it was painful, but it was not a quarrel. I went away one day and never saw her again. That was all."

The Countess looked at me gravely. "What do you call it when a man does that?"

"It depends upon the case."

"Sometimes," said the Countess in French, "it's a *lâcheté*."

"Yes, and sometimes, it's an act of wisdom."

"And sometimes," rejoined the Countess, "it's a mistake."

I shook my head.   "For me it was no mistake."

She began to laugh again.   "Caro Signore, you're a great original.   What had my poor mother done to you?".

I looked at our young Englishman, who still had his back turned to us and was staring up at the picture.   "I will tell you some other time," I said.

"I shall certainly remind you; I am very curious to know."   Then she opened and shut her fan two or three times, still looking at me.   What eyes they have!   "Tell me a little," she went on, "if I may ask without indiscretion.   Are you married?"

"No, Signora Contessa."

"Isn't that at least a mistake?"

"Do I look very unhappy?"

She dropped her head a little to one side.   "For an Englishman—no!"

"Ah," said I, laughing, "you are quite as clever as your mother."

"And they tell me that you are a great soldier," she continued; "you have lived in India.   It was very kind of you, so far away, to have remembered our poor dear Italy."

"One always remembers Italy; the distance makes

no difference. I remembered it well the day I heard of your mother's death !"

"Ah, that was a sorrow !" said the Countess. " There's not a day that I don't weep for her. But *che vuole ?* She's a saint in paradise."

" *Sicuro,*" I answered ; and I looked some time at the ground. " But tell me about yourself, dear lady," I asked at last, raising my eyes. " You have also had the sorrow of losing your husband."

"I am a poor widow, as you see. *Che vuole ?* My husband died after three years of marriage."

I waited for her to remark that the late Count Scarabelli was also a saint in paradise, but I waited in vain.

" That was like your distinguished father," I said.

"Yes, he too died young. I can't be said to have known him ; I was but of the age of my own little girl. But I weep for him all the more."

Again I was silent for a moment.

"It was in India too," I said presently, " that I heard of your mother's second marriage."

The Countess raised her eyebrows.

"In India, then, one hears of everything ! Did that news please you ?"

"Well, since you ask me—no."

"I understand that," said the Countess, looking at her open fan. "I shall not marry again like that."

"That's what your mother said to me," I ventured to observe.

She was not offended, but she rose from her seat and stood looking at me a moment. Then—

"You should not have gone away!" she exclaimed.

I stayed for another hour; it is a very pleasant house. Two or three of the men who were sitting there seemed very civil and intelligent; one of them was a major of engineers, who offered me a profusion of information upon the new organisation of the Italian army. While he talked, however, I was observing our hostess, who was talking with the others; very little, I noticed, with her young Inglese. She is altogether charming—full of frankness and freedom, of that inimitable *disinvoltura* which in an Englishwoman would be vulgar, and which in her is simply the perfection of apparent spontaneity. But for all her spontaneity she's as subtle as a needle-point, and knows tremendously well what she is

about. If she is not a consummate coquette. . . . .
What had she in her head when she said that I
should not have gone away?—Poor little Stanmer
didn't go away. I left him there at midnight.

12th.—I found him to-day sitting in the church of
Santa Croce, into which I wandered to escape from
the heat of the sun.

In the nave it was cool and dim; he was staring
at the blaze of candles on the great altar, and thinking, I am sure, of his incomparable Countess. I sat
down beside him, and after a while, as if to avoid the
appearance of eagerness, he asked me how I had
enjoyed my visit to Casa Salvi, and what I thought
of the *padrona*.

"I think half a dozen things," I said; "but I
can only tell you one now. She's an enchantress.
You shall hear the rest when we have left the
church."

"An enchantress?" repeated Stanmer, looking at
me askance.

He is a very simple youth, but who am I to
blame him?

"A charmer," I said; "a fascinatress!"

He turned away, staring at the altar-candles.

" An artist — an actress," I went on, rather brutally.

He gave me another glance.

" I think you are telling me all," he said.

" No, no, there is more."   And we sat a long time in silence.

At last he proposed that we should go out ; and we passed in the street, where the shadows had begun to stretch themselves.

" I don't know what you mean by her being an actress," he said, as we turned homeward.

" I suppose not.   Neither should I have known, if any one had said that to me."

" You are thinking about the mother," said Stanmer. " Why are you always bringing *her* in ? "

" My dear boy, the analogy is so great ; it forces itself upon me."

He stopped, and stood looking at me with his modest, perplexed young face.   I thought he was going to exclaim—" The analogy be hanged ! "—but he said after a moment—

" Well, what does it prove ? "

" I can't say it proves anything ; but it suggests a great many things."

" Be so good as to mention a few," he said, as we walked on.

" You are not sure of her yourself," I began.

" Never mind that—go on with your analogy."

" That's a part of it. You *are* very much in love with her."

" That's a part of it too, I suppose ? "

" Yes, as I have told you before. You are in love with her, and yet you can't make her out ; that's just where I was with regard to Madame de Salvi."

" And she too was an enchantress, an actress, an artist, and all the rest of it ? "

" She was the most perfect coquette I ever knew, and the most dangerous, because the most finished."

" What you mean, then, is that her daughter is a finished coquette ? "

" I rather think so."

Stanmer walked along for some moments in silence.

" Seeing that you suppose me to be a—a great admirer of the Countess," he said at last, " I am rather surprised at the freedom with which you speak of her."

I confessed that I was surprised at it myself. "But it's on account of the interest I take in you."

"I am immensely obliged to you!" said the poor boy.

"Ah, of course you don't like it. That is, you like my interest—I don't see how you can help liking that; but you don't like my freedom. That's natural enough; but, my dear young friend, I want only to help you. If a man had said to me—so many years ago—what I am saying to you, I should certainly also, at first, have thought him a great brute. But, after a little, I should have been grateful—I should have felt that he was helping me."

"You seem to have been very well able to help yourself," said Stanmer. "You tell me you made your escape."

"Yes, but it was at the cost of infinite perplexity—of what I may call keen suffering. I should like to save you all that."

"I can only repeat—it is really very kind of you."

"Don't repeat it too often, or I shall begin to think you don't mean it."

"Well," said Stanmer, "I think this, at any rate—that you take an extraordinary responsibility in trying to put a man out of conceit of a woman who, as he believes, may make him very happy."

I grasped his arm, and we stopped, going on with our talk like a couple of Florentines.

"Do you wish to marry her?"

He looked away, without meeting my eyes. "It's a great responsibility," he repeated.

"Before Heaven," I said, "I would have married the mother! You are exactly in my situation."

"Don't you think you rather overdo the analogy?" asked poor Stanmer.

"A little more, a little less—it doesn't matter. I believe you are in my shoes. But of course if you prefer it I will beg a thousand pardons and leave them to carry you where they will."

He had been looking away, but now he slowly turned his face and met my eyes. "You have gone too far to retreat; what is it you know about her?"

"About this one—nothing. But about the other —"

" I care nothing about the other ! "

" My dear fellow," I said, "they are mother and daughter—they are as like as two of Andrea's Madonnas."

" If they resemble each other, then, you were simply mistaken in the mother."

I took his arm and we walked on again ; there seemed no adequate reply to such a charge. " Your state of mind brings back my own so completely," I said presently. " You admire her—you adore her, and yet, secretly, you mistrust her. You are enchanted with her personal charm, her grace, her wit, her everything ; and yet in your private heart you are afraid of her."

" Afraid of her ? "

" Your mistrust keeps rising to the surface; you can't rid yourself of the suspicion that at the bottom of all things she is hard and cruel, and you would be immensely relieved if some one should persuade you that your suspicion is right."

Stanmer made no direct reply to this ; but before we reached the hotel he said—" What did you ever know about the mother ? "

" It's a terrible story," I answered.

He looked at me askance. " What did she do ? "

" Come to my rooms this evening and I will tell you."

He declared he would, but he never came. Exactly the way I should have acted !

14*th*.—I went again, last evening, to Casa Salvi, where I found the same little circle, with the addition of a couple of ladies. Stanmer was there, trying hard to talk to one of them, but making, I am sure, a very poor business of it. The Countess— well, the Countess was admirable. She greeted me like a friend of ten years, toward whom familiarity should not have engendered a want of ceremony ; she made me sit near her, and she asked me a dozen questions about my health and my occupations.

" I live in the past," I said. " I go into the galleries, into the old palaces and the churches. To-day I spent an hour in Michael Angelo's chapel, at San Lorenzo."

" Ah, yes, that's the past," said the Countess. " Those things are very old."

" Twenty-seven years old," I answered.

" Twenty-seven ? *Altro !* "

"I mean my own past," I said. "I went to a great many of those places with your mother."

"Ah, the pictures are beautiful," murmured the Countess, glancing at Stanmer.

"Have you lately looked at any of them?" I asked. "Have you gone to the galleries with *him?*"

She hesitated a moment, smiling. "It seems to me that your question is a little impertinent. But I think you are like that."

"A little impertinent? Never. As I say, your mother did me the honour, more than once, to accompany me to the Uffizzi."

"My mother must have been very kind to you."

"So it seemed to me at the time."

"At the time, only?"

"Well, if you prefer, so it seems to me now."

"Eh," said the Countess, "she made sacrifices."

"To what, cara Signora? She was perfectly free. Your lamented father was dead—and she had not yet contracted her second marriage."

"If she was intending to marry again, it was all the more reason she should have been careful."

I looked at her a moment; she met my eyes

gravely, over the top of her fan. "Are *you* very careful?" I said.

She dropped her fan with a certain violence. "Ah, yes, you are impertinent!"

"Ah, no," I said. "Remember that I am old enough to be your father; that I knew you when you were three years old. I may surely ask such questions. But you are right; one must do your mother justice. She was certainly thinking of her second marriage."

"You have not forgiven her that!" said the Countess, very gravely.

"Have you?" I asked, more lightly.

"I don't judge my mother. That is a mortal sin. My stepfather was very kind to me."

"I remember him," I said; "I saw him a great many times—your mother already received him."

My hostess sat with lowered eyes, saying nothing; but she presently looked up.

"She was very unhappy with my father."

"That I can easily believe. And your stepfather —is he still living?"

"He died—before my mother."

"Did he fight any more duels?"

"He was killed in a duel," said the Countess, discreetly.

It seems almost monstrous, especially as I can give no reason for it—but this announcement, instead of shocking me, caused me to feel a strange exhilaration. Most assuredly, after all these years, I bear the poor man no resentment. Of course I controlled my manner, and simply remarked to the Countess that as his fault had been, so was his punishment. I think, however, that the feeling of which I speak was at the bottom of my saying to her that I hoped that, unlike her mother's, her own brief married life had been happy.

"If it was not," she said, "I have forgotten it now."—I wonder if the late Count Scarabelli was also killed in a duel, and if his adversary . . . . Is it on the books that his adversary, as well, shall perish by the pistol? Which of those gentlemen is he, I wonder? Is it reserved for poor little Stanmer to put a bullet into him? No; poor little Stanmer, I trust, will do as I did. And yet, unfortunately for him, that woman is consummately plausible. She was wonderfully nice last evening; she was really irresistible. Such frankness and freedom,

and yet something so soft and womanly; such graceful gaiety, so much of the brightness, without any of
the stiffness, of good breeding, and over it all something so picturesquely simple and southern. She is
a perfect Italian. But she comes honestly by it.
After the talk I have just jotted down she changed
her place, and the conversation for half-an-hour was
general. Stanmer indeed said very little; partly, I
suppose, because he is shy of talking a foreign tongue.
Was I like that—was I so constantly silent? I
suspect I was when I was perplexed, and Heaven
knows that very often my perplexity was extreme.
Before I went away I had a few more words *tête-à-
tête* with the Countess.

"I hope you are not leaving Florence yet," she
said; "you will stay a while longer?"

I answered that I came only for a week, and that
my week was over.

"I stay on from day to day, I am so much interested."

"Eh, it's the beautiful moment. I'm glad our city
pleases you!"

"Florence pleases me—and I take a paternal
interest in our young friend," I added, glancing

at Stanmer. "I have become very fond of him."

"*Bel tipo inglese*," said my hostess. "And he is very intelligent; he has a beautiful mind."

She stood there resting her smile and her clear, expressive eyes upon me.

"I don't like to praise him too much," I rejoined, "lest I should appear to praise myself; he reminds me so much of what I was at his age. If your beautiful mother were to come to life for an hour she would see the resemblance."

She gave me a little amused stare.

"And yet you don't look at all like him!"

"Ah, you didn't know me when I was twenty five. I was very handsome! And, moreover, it isn't that, it's the mental resemblance. I was ingenuous, candid, trusting, like him."

"Trusting? I remember my mother once telling me that you were the most suspicious and jealous of men!"

"I fell into a suspicious mood, but I was, fundamentally, not in the least addicted to thinking evil. I couldn't easily imagine any harm of any one."

"And so you mean that Mr. Stanmer is in a suspicious mood?"

"Well, I mean that his situation is the same as mine."

The Countess gave me one of her serious looks.

"Come," she said, "what was it—this famous situation of yours? I have heard you mention it before."

"Your mother might have told you, since she occasionally did me the honour to speak of me."

"All my mother ever told me was that you were a sad puzzle to her."

At this, of course, I laughed out—I laugh still as I write it.

"Well, then, that was my situation—I was a sad puzzle to a very clever woman."

"And you mean, therefore, that I am a puzzle to poor Mr. Stanmer?"

"He is racking his brains to make you out. Remember it was you who said he was intelligent."

She looked round at him, and as fortune would have it, his appearance at that moment quite confirmed my assertion. He was lounging back in his chair with an air of indolence rather too marked for a drawing-room, and staring at the ceiling with the expression of a man who has just been asked a conundrum. Madame Scarabelli seemed struck with his attitude.

"Don't you see," I said, "he can't read the riddle?"

"You yourself," she answered, "said he was incapable of thinking evil. I should be sorry to have him think any evil of *me*."

And she looked straight at me—seriously, appealingly—with her beautiful candid brow.

I inclined myself, smiling, in a manner which might have meant—

"How could that be possible?"

"I have a great esteem for him," she went on; "I want him to think well of me. If I am a puzzle to him, do me a little service. Explain me to him."

"Explain you, dear lady?"

"You are older and wiser than he. Make him understand me."

She looked deep into my eyes for a moment, and then she turned away.

26th.—I have written nothing for a good many days, but meanwhile I have been half a dozen times to Casa Salvi. I have seen a good deal also of my young friend—had a good many walks and talks with him. I have proposed to him to come with me to Venice for a fortnight, but he won't listen to the idea of leaving Florence. He is very happy in spite of his doubts, and I confess that in the perception of his happiness I have lived over again my own. This is so much the case that when, the other day, he at last made up his mind to ask me to tell him the wrong that Madame de Salvi had done me, I rather checked his curiosity. I told him that if he was bent upon knowing I would satisfy him, but that it seemed a pity, just now, to indulge in painful imagery.

. "But I thought you wanted so much to put me out of conceit of our friend."

"I admit I am inconsistent, but there are various reasons for it. In the first place—it's obvious—I am open to the charge of playing a double game. I profess an admiration for the Countess Scarabelli, for I accept her hospitality, and at the same time I attempt to poison your mind; isn't that the proper expression ? .I can't exactly make up my mind to that, though my admiration for the Countess and my desire to prevent you from taking a foolish step are equally sincere.   And then, in the second place you seem to me on the whole so happy ! One hesitates to destroy an illusion, no matter how pernicious, that is so delightful while it lasts.   These are the rare moments of life.   To be young and ardent, in the midst of an Italian spring, and to believe in the moral perfection of a beautiful woman—what an admirable situation !   Float with the current; I'll stand on the brink and watch you."

"Your real reason is that you feel you have no case against the poor lady," said Stanmer.   "You admire her as much as I do."

"I just admitted that I admired her.   I never said she was a vulgar flirt ; her mother was an absolutely scientific one.   Heaven knows I admired that !   It's a nice point, however, how much one is bound in honour not to warn a young friend against a dangerous woman because one also has relations of civility with the lady."

"In such a case," said Stanmer, "I would break off my relations."

I looked at him, and I think I laughed.

"Are you jealous of me, by chance ?"

He shook his head emphatically.

"Not in the least; I like to see you there, because your conduct contradicts your words."

"I have always said that the Countess is fascinating."

"Otherwise," said Stanmer, "in the case you speak of I would give the lady notice."

"Give her notice?"

"Mention to her that you regard her with suspicion, and that you propose to do your best to rescue a simple-minded youth from her wiles. That would be more loyal." And he began to laugh again.

It is not the first time he has laughed at me; but I have never minded it, because I have always understood it.

"Is that what you recommend me to say to the Countess?" I asked.

"Recommend you!" he exclaimed, laughing again; "I recommend nothing. I may be the victim to be rescued, but I am at least not a partner to the conspiracy. Besides," he added in a moment, "the Countess knows your state of mind."

"Has she told you so?"

Stanmer hesitated.

"She has begged me to listen to everything you may say against her. She declares that she has a good conscience."

"Ah," said I, "she's an accomplished woman!"

And it is indeed very clever of her to take that tone. Stanmer afterwards assured me explicitly that he has never given her a hint of the liberties I have taken in conversation with—what shall I call it?—with her moral nature; she has guessed them for herself. She must hate me intensely, and yet her manner has always been so charming to me! She is truly an accomplished woman!

May 4th.—I have stayed away from Casa Salvi for a week, but I have lingered on in Florence, under a mixture of impulses. I have had it on my conscience not to go near the Countess again—and yet from the moment she is aware of the way I feel about her, it is open war. There need be no scruples on either side. She is as free to use every possible art to entangle poor Stanmer more closely as I am to clip her fine-spun meshes. Under the circumstances, however, we naturally shouldn't meet very cordially. But as regards her meshes, why, after all, should I clip them? It would really be very

interesting to see Stanmer swallowed up. I should
like to see how he would agree with her after she
had devoured him—(to what vulgar imagery, by the
way, does curiosity reduce a man!) Let him finish
the story in his own way, as I finished it in mine. It
is the same story; but why, a quarter of a century
later, should it have the same *dénoûment?* Let him
make his own *dénoûment.*

5*th.*—Hang it, however, I don't want the poor boy
to be miserable.

6*th.*—Ah, but did my *dénoûment* then prove such
a happy one?

7*th.*—He came to my room late last night; he was
much excited.

"What was it she did to you?" he asked.

I answered him first with another question. "Have
you quarrelled with the Countess?"

But he only repeated his own. "What was it she
did to you?"

"Sit down and I'll tell you." And he sat there
beside the candle, staring at me. "There was a man
always there—Count Camerino."

"The man she married?"

"The man she married. I was very much in love

with her, and yet I didn't trust her. I was sure that she lied ; I believed that she could be cruel. Nevertheless, at moments, she had a charm which made it pure pedantry to be conscious of her faults ; and while these moments lasted I would have done anything for her. Unfortunately, they didn't last long. But you know what I mean; am I not describing the Scarabelli ? "

" The Countess Scarabelli never lied ! " cried Stanmer.

" That's just what I would have said to any one who should have made the insinuation ! But I suppose you are not asking me the question you put to me just now from dispassionate curiosity."

" A man may want to know ! " said the innocent fellow.

I couldn't help laughing out. " This, at any rate, is my story. Camerino was always there ; he was a sort of fixture in the house. If I had moments of dislike for the divine Bianca, I had no moments of liking for him. And yet he was a very agreeable fellow, very civil, very intelligent, not in the least disposed to make a quarrel with me. The trouble of course was simply that I was jealous of him. I don't know, however, on what ground I could have quarrelled with him, for I had no definite rights. I can't say what I expected—I can't say what, as the matter stood, I was prepared to do. With my name and my prospects, I might perfectly have offered her my hand. I am not sure that she would have accepted it—I am by no means clear that she wanted that. But she wanted, wanted keenly, to attach me to her; she wanted to have me about. I should have been capable of giving up everything— England, my career, my family—simply to devote myself to her, to live near her and see her every day."

"Why didn't you do it, then?" asked Stanmer.

"Why don't you?"

"To be a proper rejoinder to my question," he said, rather neatly, "yours should be asked twenty-five years hence."

"It remains perfectly true that at a given moment I was capable of doing as I say. That was what she wanted—a rich, susceptible, credulous, convenient young Englishman established near her *en permanence*. And yet," I added, "I must do her complete justice. I honestly believe she was fond of me." At this

Stanmer got up and walked to the window; he stood looking out a moment, and then he turned round. "You know she was older than I," I went on. "Madame Scarabelli is older than you. One day in the garden, her mother asked me in an angry tone why I disliked Camerino; for I had been at no pains to conceal my feeling about him, and something had just happened to bring it out. 'I dislike him,' I said, 'because you like him so much.' 'I assure you I don't like him,' she answered. 'He has all the appearance of being your lover,' I retorted. It was a brutal speech, certainly, but any other man in my place would have made it. She took it very strangely; she turned pale, but she was not indignant. 'How can he be my lover after what he has done?' she asked. 'What has he done?' She hesitated a good while, then she said: 'He killed my husband.' 'Good heavens!' I cried, 'and you receive him?' Do you know what she said? She said, '*Che vuole?*'"

"Is that all?" asked Stanmer.

"No; she went on to say that Camerino had killed Count Salvi in a duel, and she admitted that her husband's jealousy had been the occasion of it.

The Count, it appeared, was a monster of jealousy
—he had led her a dreadful life.   He himself, meanwhile, had been anything but irreproachable ; he had
done a mortal injury to a man of whom he pretended
to be a friend, and this affair had become notorious.
The gentleman in question had demanded satisfaction
for his outraged honour ; but for some reason or
other (the Countess, to do her justice, did not tell
me that her husband was a coward), he had not as yet
obtained it.   The duel with Camerino had come on
first ; in an access of jealous fury the Count had
struck Camerino in the face ; and this outrage, I
know not how justly, was deemed expiable before
the other.   By an extraordinary arrangement (the
Italians have certainly no sense of fair play), the
other man was allowed to be Camarino's second.
The duel was fought with swords, and the Count
received a wound of which, though at first it was
not expected to be fatal, he died on the following
day.   The matter was hushed up as much as possible
for the sake of the Countess's good name, and so
successfully that it was presently observed that,
among the public, the other gentleman had the
credit of having put his blade through M. de Salvi.

This gentleman took a fancy not to contradict the impression, and it was allowed to subsist. So long as *he* consented, it was of course in Camerino's interest not to contradict it, as it left him much more free to keep up his intimacy with the Countess."

Stanmer had listened to all this with extreme attention. "Why didn't *she* contradict it ?"

I shrugged my shoulders. "I am bound to believe it was for the same reason. I was horrified, at any rate, by the whole story. I was extremely shocked at the Countess's want of dignity in continuing to see the man by whose hand her husband had fallen."

"The husband had been a great brute, and it was not known," said Stanmer.

"Its not being known made no difference. And as for Salvi having been a brute, that is but a way of saying that his wife, and the man whom his wife subsequently married, didn't like him."

Stanmer looked extremely meditative ; his eyes were fixed on mine. "Yes, that marriage is hard to get over. It was not becoming."

"Ah," said I, "what a long breath I drew when I heard of it ! I remember the place and the hour. It was at a hill-station in India, seven years after I had left Florence. The post brought me some English papers, and in one of them was a letter from Italy, with a lot of so-called 'fashionable intelligence.' There, among various scandals in high-life, and other delectable items, I read that the Countess Bianca Salvi, famous for some years as the presiding genius of the most agreeable *salon* in Florence, was about to bestow her hand upon Count Camerino, a distinguished Bolognese. Ah, my dear boy, it was a tremendous escape! I had been ready to marry the woman who was capable of that! But my instinct had warned me, and I had trusted my instinct."

"'Instinct's everything,' as Falstaff says!" And Stanmer began to laugh. "Did you tell Madame de Salvi that your instinct was against her?"

"No; I told her that she frightened me, shocked me, horrified me."

"That's about the same thing. And what did she say?"

"She asked me what I would have? I called her friendship with Camerino a scandal, and she answered that her husband had been a brute. Besides, no one knew it; therefore it was no scandal. Just *your* argument! I retorted that this was odious reasoning, and that she had no moral sense. We had a passionate argument, and I declared I would never see her again. In the heat of my displeasure I left Florence, and I kept my vow. I never saw her again."

"You couldn't have been much in love with her," said Stanmer.

"I was not—three months after."

"If you had been you would have come back—three days after."

"So doubtless it seems to you. All I can say is that it was the great effort of my life. Being a military man, I have had on various occasions to face the enemy. But it was not then I needed my resolution; it was when I left Florence in a post-chaise."

Stanmer turned about the room two or three times, and then he said: "I don't understand! I don't understand why she should have told you that Camerino had killed her husband. It could only damage her."

"She was afraid it would damage her more that I should think he was her lover. She wished to say the thing that would most effectually persuade me that he was not her lover—that he could never be.

And then she wished to get the credit of being very frank."

"Good heavens, how you must have analysed her!" cried my companion, staring.

"There is nothing so analytic as disillusionment. But there it is. She married Camerino."

"Yes, I don't like that," said Stanmer. He was silent a while, and then he added—"Perhaps she wouldn't have done so if you had remained."

He has a little innocent way! "Very likely she would have dispensed with the ceremony," I answered dryly.

"Upon my word," he said, "you *have* analysed her!"

"You ought to be grateful to me. I have done for you what you seem unable to do for yourself."

"I don't see any Camerino in my case," he said.

"Perhaps among those gentlemen I can find one for you."

"Thank you," he cried; "I'll take care of that myself!" And he went away—satisfied, I hope.

10*th*.—He's an obstinate little wretch; it irritates me to see him sticking to it. Perhaps he is looking for his Camerino. I shall leave him at any rate to his fate; it is growing insupportably hot.

11*th.*—I went this evening to bid farewell to the Scarabelli. There was no one there; she was alone in her great dusky drawing-room, which was lighted only by a couple of candles, with the immense windows open over the garden. She was dressed in white; she was deucedly pretty. She asked me of course why I had been so long without coming.

"I think you say that only for form," I answered. "I imagine you know."

"*Chè!* what have I done?"

"Nothing at all. You are too wise for that."

She looked at me a while. "I think you are a little crazy."

"Ah no, I am only too sane. I have too much reason rather than too little."

"You have at any rate what we call a fixed idea."

"There is no harm in that so long as it's a good one."

"But yours is abominable!" she exclaimed with a laugh.

"Of course you can't like me or my ideas. All things considered, you have treated me with wonderful kindness, and I thank you and kiss your hands. I leave Florence to-morrow."

"I won't say I'm sorry !" she said, laughing again. "But I am very glad to have seen you. I always wondered about you. You are a curiosity."

"Yes, you must find me so. A man who can resist your charms ! The fact is, I can't. This evening you are enchanting ; and it is the first time I have been alone with you."

She gave no heed to this ; she turned away. But in a moment she came back, and stood looking at me, and her beautiful solemn eyes seemed to shine in the dimness of the room.

"How *could* you treat my mother so ?" she asked.

"Treat her so ?"

"How could you desert the most charming woman in the world ?"

"It was not a case of desertion ; and if it had been it seems to me she was consoled."

At this moment there was the sound of a step in the ante-chamber, and I saw that the Countess perceived it to be Stanmer's.

"That wouldn't have happened," she murmured. "My poor mother needed a protector."

Stanmer came in, interrupting our talk, and looking at me, I thought, with a little air of bravado. He must think me indeed a tiresome, meddlesome bore; and upon my word, turning it all over, I wonder at his docility. After all, he's five-and-twenty—and yet, I *must* add, it *does* irritate me—the way he sticks! He was followed in a moment by two or three of the regular Italians, and I made my visit short.

"Good-bye, Countess," I said; and she gave me her hand in silence. "Do *you* need a protector?" I added, softly.

She looked at me from head to foot, and then, almost angrily—

"Yes, Signore."

But, to deprecate her anger, I kept her hand an instant, and then bent my venerable head and kissed it. I think I appeased her.

·BOLOGNA, 14*th.*—I left Florence on the 11th, and have been here these three days. Delightful old Italian town—but it lacks the charm of my Florentine secret.

I wrote that last entry five days ago, late at night, after coming back from Casa Salvi. I afterwards fell asleep in my chair; the night was half over when I woke up. Instead of going to bed, I stood a long time at the window, looking out at the river. It was a warm, still night, and the first faint streaks of sunrise were in the sky. Presently I heard a slow footstep beneath my window, and looking down, made out by the aid of a street-lamp that Stanmer was but just coming home. I called to him to come to my rooms, and, after an interval, he made his appearance.

"I want to bid you good-bye," I said; "I shall depart in the morning. Don't go to the trouble of saying you are sorry. Of course you are not; I must have bullied you immensely."

He made no attempt to say he was sorry, but he said he was very glad to have made my acquaintance.

"Your conversation," he said, with his little innocent air, "has been very suggestive."

"Have you found Camerino?" I asked, smiling.

"I have given up the search."

"Well," I said, "some day when you find that you have made a great mistake, remember I told you so."

He looked for a minute as if he were trying to anticipate that day by the exercise of his reason.

"Has it ever occurred to you that *you* may have made a great mistake?"

"Oh yes; everything occurs to one sooner or later."

That's what I said ·to him ; but I didn't say that the question, pointed by his candid young countenance, had, for the moment, a greater force than it had ever had before.

And then he asked me whether, as things had turned out, I myself had been so especially happy.

PARIS, *December* 17*th.*—A note from young Stanmer, whom I saw in Florence—a remarkable little note, dated Rome, and worth transcribing.

"*My Dear General,—I have it at heart to tell you that I was married a week ago to the Countess Salvi-Scarabelli. You talked me into a great muddle; but a month after that it was all very clear. Things that involve a risk are like the Christian faith; they must be seen from the inside.—Yours ever,* E. S.

"P.S.—*A fig for analogies unless you can find an analogy for my happiness!*"

His happiness makes him very clever. I hope it will last!—I mean his cleverness, not his happiness.

LONDON, *April* 19*th*, 1877.—Last night, at Lady

H——'s, I met Edmund Stanmer, who married Bianca Salvi's daughter. I heard the other day that they had come to England. A handsome young fellow, with a fresh contented face. He reminded me of Florence, which I didn't pretend to forget; but it was rather awkward, for I remember I used to disparage that woman to him. I had a complete theory about her. But he didn't seem at all stiff; on the contrary, he appeared to enjoy our encounter. I asked him if his wife were there. I had to do that.

"Oh, yes, she's in one of the other rooms. Come and make her acquaintance; I want you to know her."

"You forget that I do know her."

"Oh, no, you don't; you never did." And he gave a little significant laugh.

I didn't feel like facing the *ci-devant* Scarabelli at that moment; so I said that I was leaving the house, but that I would do myself the honour of calling upon his wife. We talked for a minute of something else, and then, suddenly, breaking off and looking at me, he laid his hand on my arm. I must do him the justice to say that he looks felicitous.

"Depend upon it, you were wrong!" he said.

"My dear young friend," I answered, "imagine the alacrity with which I concede it."

Something else again was spoken of, but in an instant he repeated his movement.

"Depend upon it you were wrong."

"I am sure the Countess has forgiven me," I said, "and in that case you ought to bear no grudge. As I have had the honour to say, I will call upon her immediately."

"I was not alluding to my wife," he answered. "I was thinking of your own story."

"My own story?"

"So many years ago. Was it not rather a mistake?"

I looked at him a moment; he's positively rosy.

"That's not a question to solve in a London crush."

And I turned away.

22nd.—I haven't yet called on the *ci-devant;* I am afraid of finding her at home. And that boy's words have been thrumming in my ears—"Depend upon it you were wrong. Wasn't it rather a mistake?" *Was* I wrong—*was* it a mistake? Was I too cautious—too suspicious—too logical? Was it really a protector she needed—a man who might have helped her? Would it have been for his benefit to believe in her, and was her fault only that I had forsaken her? Was the poor woman very unhappy? God forgive me, how the questions come crowding in! If I marred her happiness, I certainly didn't make my own. And I might have made it—eh? That's a charming discovery for a man of my age!

BENVOLIO.

I.

ONCE upon a time (as if he had lived in a fairy-tale) there was a very interesting young man. This is not a fairy-tale, and yet our young man was in some respects as pretty a fellow as any fairy prince. I call him interesting because his type of character is one I have always found it profitable to observe. If you fail to consider him so, I shall be willing to confess that the fault is mine and not his; I shall have told my story with too little skill.

His name was Benvolio; that is, it was not; but we shall call him so for the sake both of convenience and of picturesqueness. He was about to enter upon the third decade of our mortal span; he had a little property, and he followed no regular profession.

His personal appearance was in the highest degree prepossessing. Having said this, it were perhaps well that I should let you—you especially, madam—suppose that he exactly corresponded to your ideal of manly beauty; but I am bound to explain definitely wherein it was that he resembled a fairy prince, and I need furthermore to make a record of certain little peculiarities and anomalies in which it is probable that your brilliant conception would be deficient. Benvolio was slim and fair, with clustering locks, remarkably fine eyes, and such a frank, expressive smile that on the journey through life it was almost as serviceable to its owner as the magic key, or the enchanted ring, or the wishing-cap, or any other bauble of necromantic properties. Unfortunately this charming smile was not always at his command, and its place was sometimes occupied by a very perverse and dusky frown, which rendered the young man no service whatever—not even that of frightening people; for though it expressed extreme irritation and impatience, it was characterized by the brevity of contempt, and the only revenge upon disagreeable things and offensive people that it seemed to express a desire for on Benvolio's part was that of forgetting

and ignoring them with the utmost possible celerity.
It never made any one tremble, though now and then
it perhaps made irritable people murmur an impreca-
tion or two. You might have supposed from Benvolio's manner, when he was in good humour (which
was the greater part of the time), from his brilliant,
intelligent glance, from his easy, irresponsible step,
and in especial from the sweet, clear, lingering, caress-
ing tone of his voice—the voice as it were of a man
whose fortune has been made for him, and who as-
sumes, a trifle egotistically, that the rest of the world
is equally at leisure to share with him the sweets of
life, to pluck the wayside flowers, and chase the
butterflies afield—you might have supposed, I say,
from all this luxurious assurance of demeanour, that
our hero really had the wishing-cap sitting invisible
on his handsome brow, or was obliged only to close
his knuckles together a moment to exert an effective
pressure upon the magic ring. The young man, I
have said, was a mixture of inconsistencies; I may
say more exactly that he was a tissue of contradictions. He did possess the magic ring, in a certain
fashion; he possessed in other words the poetic
imagination. Everything that fancy could do for

him was done in perfection. It gave him immense satisfactions; it transfigured the world; it made very common objects sometimes seem radiantly beautiful, and it converted beautiful ones into infinite sources of intoxication. Benvolio had what is called the poetic temperament. It is rather out of fashion to describe a man in these terms; but I believe, in spite of much evidence to the contrary, that there are poets still; and if we may call a spade a spade, why should we not call such a person as Benvolio a poet?

These contradictions that I speak of ran through his whole nature, and they were perfectly apparent in his habits, in his manners, in his conversation, and even in his physiognomy. It was as if the souls of two very different men had been placed together to make the voyage of life in the same boat, and had agreed for convenience' sake to take the helm in alternation. The helm, with Benvolio, was always the imagination; but in his different moods it worked very differently. To an acute observer his face itself would have betrayed these variations; and it is certain that his dress, his talk, his way of spending his time, one day and another, abundantly indicated them. Sometimes he looked very young—rosy,

radiant, blooming, younger than his years. Then
suddenly, as the light struck his head in a particular
manner, you would see that his golden locks contained a surprising number of silver threads; and
with your attention quickened by this discovery, you
would proceed to detect something grave and discreet
in his smile—something vague and ghostly, like the
dim adumbration of the darker half of the lunar
disk. You might have met Benvolio, in certain states
of mind, dressed like a man of the highest fashion—
wearing his hat on his ear, a rose in his button-hole,
a wonderful intaglio or an antique Syracusan coin, by
way of a pin, in his cravat. Then, on the morrow,
you would have espied him braving the sunshine in
a rusty scholar's coat, with his hat pulled over his
brow—a costume wholly at odds with flowers and
gems. It was all a matter of fancy; but his fancy
was a weather-cock, and faced east or west as the
wind blew. His conversation matched his coat and
breeches; he talked one day the talk of the town;
he chattered, he gossipped, he asked questions and
told stories; you would have said that he was a
charming fellow for a dinner-party or the pauses of a
cotillon. The next he either talked philosophy or

politics, or said nothing at all; he was absent and
indifferent; he was thinking his own thoughts; he
had a book in his pocket, and evidently he was
composing one in his head. At home he lived
in two chambers. One was an immense room,
hung with pictures, lined with books, draped with
rugs and tapestries, decorated with a multitude
of ingenious devices (for of all these things he
was very fond); the other, his sleeping-room, was
almost as bare as a monastic cell. It had a meagre
little strip of carpet on the floor, and a dozen well-
thumbed volumes of classic poets and sages on
the mantelshelf. On the wall hung three or four
coarsely-engraved portraits of the most exemplary
of these worthies; these were the only orna-
ments. But the room had the charm of a great
window, in a deep embrasure, looking out upon a
tangled, silent, moss-grown garden, and in the embrasure stood the little ink-blotted table at which
Benvolio did most of his poetic scribbling. The
windows of his sumptuous sitting-room commanded
a wide public square, where people were always
passing and lounging, where military music used to
play on vernal nights, and half the life of the great

town went forward. At the risk of your thinking our
hero a sad idler, I will say that he spent an inordinate
amount of time in gazing out of these windows (in
either direction) with his elbows on the sill. The
garden did not belong to the house which he in-
habited, but to a neighbouring one, and the proprietor, a graceless old miser, was very chary of
permits to visit his domain. But Benvolio's fancy
used to wander through the alleys without stirring
the long arms of the untended plants, and to bend
over the heavy-headed flowers without leaving a foot-
print on their beds. It was here that his happiest
thoughts came to him—that inspiration (as we may
say, speaking of a man of the poetic temperament),
descended upon him in silence, and for certain divine,
appreciable moments stood poised along the course
of his scratching quill. It was not, however, that
he had not spent some very charming hours in the
larger, richer apartment. He used to receive his
friends there—sometimes in great numbers, sometimes at boisterous, many-voiced suppers, which
lasted far into the night. When these entertain-
ments were over he never made a direct transition
to his little scholar's cell. He went out and wandered

for an hour through the dark, sleeping streets of the town, ridding himself of the fumes of wine, and feeling not at all tipsy, but intensely, portentously sober. More than once, when he had come back and prepared to go to bed, he saw the first faint glow of dawn trembling upward over the tree-tops of his garden. His friends, coming to see him, often found the greater room empty, and advancing, rapped at the door of his chamber. But he frequently kept quiet, not desiring in the least to see them, knowing exactly what they were going to say, and not thinking it worth hearing. Then, hearing them stride away, and the outer door close behind them, he would come forth and take a turn in his slippers, over his Persian carpets, and glance out of the window and see his defeated visitant stand scratching his chin in the sunny square. After this he would laugh lightly to himself—as is said to be the habit of the scribbling tribe in moments of production.

Although he had many relatives he enjoyed extreme liberty. His family was so large, his brothers and sisters were so numerous, that he could absent himself and be little missed. Sometimes he used this privilege freely ; he tired of people whom he had seen very often, and he had seen, of course, a great deal of his family. At other moments he was extremely domestic; he suddenly found solitude depressing, and it seemed to him that if one sought society as a refuge, one needed to be on familiar terms with it, and that with no one was familiarity so natural as among people who had grown up at a common fireside. Nevertheless it frequently occurred to him—for sooner or later everything occurred to him—that he was too independent and irresponsible ; that he would be happier if he had a little golden ball and chain tied to his ankle. His curiosity about all things—life and love and art and truth—was great, and his theory was to satisfy it as freely as might be ; but as the years went by this pursuit of impartial science appeared to produce a singular result. He became conscious of an intellectual condition similar to that of a palate which has lost its relish. To a man with a disordered appetite all things taste alike, and so it seemed to Benvolio that the gustatory faculty of his mind was losing its keenness. It had still its savoury moments, its feasts and its holidays ; but, on the whole, the spectacle of human life was

growing flat and stale. This is simply a wordy way
of expressing that comprehensive fact—Benvolio was
blasé. He knew it, he knew it betimes, and he re-
gretted it acutely. He believed that the mind can
keep its freshness to the last, and that it is only fools
that are overbored. There was a way of never being
bored, and the wise man's duty was to find it out.
One of its rudiments, he believed, was that one grows
tired of one's self sooner than of anything else in the
world. Idleness, every one admitted, was the greatest
of follies ; but idleness was subtle, and exacted tribute
under a hundred plausible disguises. One was often
idle when one seemed to be ardently occupied ; one
was always idle when one's occupation had not a high
aim. One was idle therefore when one was working
simply for one's self. Curiosity for curiosity's sake,
art for art's sake, these were essentially broken-winded
steeds. Ennui was at the end of everything that did
not multiply our relations with life. To multiply his
relations, therefore, Benvolio reflected, should be the
wise man's aim. Poor Benvolio had to reflect on
this, because, as I say, he was a poet and not a man
of action. A fine fellow of the latter stamp would
have solved the problem without knowing it, and

bequeathed to his fellow men not frigid formulas but vivid examples. But Benvolio had often said to himself that he was born to imagine great things—not to do them ; and he had said this by no means sadly, for on the whole he was very well content with his portion. Imagine them he determined he would, and on a magnificent scale. He would multiply his labours at least, and they should be very serious ones. He would cultivate great ideas, he would enunciate great truths, he would write immortal verses. In all this there was a large amount of talent and a liberal share of ambition. I will not say that Benvolio was a man of genius; it may seem to make the distinction too cheap ; but he was at any rate a man with an intellectual passion; and if, being near him, you had been able to listen intently enough, he would, like the great people of his craft, have seemed to emit something of that vague magical murmur—the voice of the infinite—which lurks in the involutions of a sea-shell. He himself, by the way, had once made use of this little simile, and had written a poem in which it was melodiously set forth that the poetic minds scattered about the world correspond to the little shells one picks up on the beach, all resonant with the echo of ocean. The whole thing was of course rounded off with the sands of time, the waves of history, and other harmonious conceits.

II

BUT (as you are naturally expecting to hear), Benvolio knew perfectly well that there is one relation with life which is a better antidote to ennui than any other—the relation established with a charming woman. Benvolio was of course in love. Who was his mistress, you ask (I flatter myself with some impatience), and was she pretty, was she kind, was he successful? Hereby hangs my tale, which I must relate in due form.

Benvolio's mistress was a lady whom (as I cannot tell you her real name) it will be quite in keeping to speak of as the Countess. The Countess was a young widow, who had some time since divested herself of her mourning weeds—which indeed she had never worn but very lightly. She was rich, extremely pretty, and free to do as she listed. She was passionately fond of pleasure and admiration,

and they gushed forth at her feet in unceasing
streams. Her beauty was not of the conventional
type, but it was dazzlingly brilliant; few faces were
more expressive, more fascinating. Hers was never
the same for two days together; it reflected her
momentary circumstances with extraordinary vivid-
ness, and in knowing her you had the advantage of
knowing a dozen different women. She was clever
and accomplished, and had the credit of being perfectly amiable; indeed it was difficult to imagine a
person combining a greater number of the precious
gifts of nature and fortune. She represented felicity,
gaiety, success; she was made to charm, to play a
part, to exert a sway. She lived in a great house,
behind high verdure-muffled walls, where other
Countesses, in other years, had played a part no less
brilliant. It was an antiquated quarter, into which
the tide of commerce had lately begun to roll heavily;
but the turbid wave of trade broke in vain against
the Countess's enclosure, and if in her garden and
her drawing-room you heard the deep uproar of the
city, it was only as a vague undertone to sweeter
things—to music, and witty talk, and tender colloquy.
There was something very striking in this little oasis

of luxury and privacy, in the midst of common toil
and traffic.

Benvolio was a great deal at this lady's house ; he
rarely desired better entertainment. I spoke just
now of privacy ; but privacy was not what he found
there, nor what he wished to find. He went there
when he wished to learn with the least trouble what
was going on in the world ; for the talk of the people
the Countess generally had about her was an epitome
of the gossip, the rumours, the interests, the hopes
and fears, of polite society. She was a thoroughly
liberal hostess ; all she asked was to be entertained ;
if you would contribute to the common fund of
amusement, of discussion, you were a welcome guest.
Sooner or later, among your fellow-guests, you encountered every one of consequence. There were frivolous
people and wise people ; people whose fortune was in
their pockets and people whose fortune was in their
brains ; people deeply concerned in public affairs and
people concerned only with the fit of their garments
or with the effect upon the company of the announcement of their names. Benvolio, with his taste for a
large and various social spectacle, appreciated all this ;
but he was best pleased, as a general thing, when he

found the Countess alone. This was often his fortune, for the simple reason that when the Countess
expected him she invariably caused herself to be
refused to every one else. This is almost an answer
to your inquiry whether Benvolio was successful in
his suit. As yet, strictly speaking, there was no suit ;
Benvolio had never made love to the Countess. This
sounds very strange, but it is nevertheless true. He
was in love with her ; he thought her the most charming creature conceivable ; he spent hours with her
alone by her own orders ; he had had opportunity—he
had been up to his neck in opportunity—and yet he
had never said to her, as would have seemed so natural,
"Dear Countess, I beseech you to be my wife." If
you are surprised, I may also confide to you that the
Countess was ; and surprise under the circumstances
very easily became displeasure. It is by no means
certain that if Benvolio had made the little speech we
have just imagined, the Countess would have fallen
into his arms, confessed to an answering flame, and
rung in *finis* to our tale, with the wedding-bells. But
she nevertheless expected him in civility to pay her
this supreme compliment. Her answer would be—
what it might be ; but his silence was a permanent

offence. Every man, roughly speaking, had asked
the Countess to marry him, and every man had been
told that she was much obliged, but had not been
thinking of changing her condition. But here, with
the one man who failed to ask her, she was per-
petually thinking of it, and this negative quality in
Benvolio was more present to her mind, gave her
more to think about, than all the positiveness of her
other suitors. The truth was she liked Benvolio
extremely, and his independence rendered him excellent service. The Countess had a very lively fancy,
and she had fingered, nimbly enough, the volume of
the young man's merits. She was by nature a trifle
cold ; she rarely lost her head ; she measured each
step as she took it ; she had had little fancies and
incipient passions ; but on the whole she had thought
much more about love than felt it. She had often
tried to form an image of the sort of man it would be
well for her to love—for so it was she expressed it.
She had succeeded but indifferently, and her imagination had never found a pair of wings until the day
she met Benvolio. Then it seemed to her that her
quest was ended—her prize gained. This nervous,
ardent, deep-eyed youth struck her as the harmonious

counterpart of her own facile personality. This conviction rested with the Countess on a fine sense of
propriety which it would be vain to attempt to analyze ;
he was different from herself and from the other men
who surrounded her, and she valued him as a specimen
of a rare and distinguished type. In the old days she
would have appointed him to be her minstrel or her
jester—it is to be feared that poor Benvolio would
have figured rather dismally in the latter capacity;
and at present a woman who was in her own right
a considerable social figure, might give such a man a
place in her train as an illustrious husband. I don't
know how good a judge the Countess was of such
matters, but she believed that the world would hear
of Benvolio. She had beauty, ancestry, money,
luxury, but she had not genius ; and if genius was to
be had, why not secure it, and complete the list ?
This is doubtless a rather coarse statement of the
Countess's argument ; but you have it thrown in
gratis, as it were ; for all I am bound to tell you is
that this charming young woman took a fancy to this
clever young man, and that she used to cry sometimes
for a quarter of a minute when she imagined he was
indifferent to her. Her tears were wasted, because

he really cared for her—more even than she would
have imagined if she had taken a favourable view of
the case. But Benvolio, I cannot too much repeat,
was an exceedingly complex character, and there
was many a lapse in the logic of his conduct. The
Countess charmed him, excited him, interested him ;
he did her abundant justice—more than justice ; but
at the end of all he felt that she failed to satisfy him.
If a man could have half a dozen wives—and Benvolio
had once maintained, poetically, that he ought to
have—the Countess would do very well for one of
them—possibly even for the best of them. But she
would not serve for all seasons and all moods ; she
needed a complement, an alternative — what the
French call a *repoussoir*. One day he was going to
see her, knowing that he was expected. There was
to be a number of other people—in fact, a very brilliant assembly ; but Benvolio knew that a certain
touch of the hand, a certain glance of the eye, a
certain caress of the voice, would be reserved for him
alone. Happy Benvolio, you will say, to be going
about the world with such charming secrets as this
locked up in his young heart ! Happy Benvolio indeed ; but mark how he trifled with his happiness.

He went to the Countess's gate, but he went no
further; he stopped, stood there a moment, frowning
intensely, and biting the finger of his glove; then
suddenly he turned and strode away in the opposite
direction. He walked and walked and left the town
behind him. He went his way till he reached the
country, and here he bent his steps toward a little
wood which he knew very well, and whither indeed,
on a spring afternoon, when she had taken a fancy to
play at shepherd and shepherdess, he had once come
with the Countess. He flung himself on the grass,
on the edge of the wood—not in the same place
where he had lain at the Countess's feet, pulling son-
nets out of his pocket and reading them one by one;
a little stream flowed beside him; opposite, the sun
was declining; the distant city lay before him, lifting
its towers and chimneys against the reddening western
sky. The twilight fell and deepened and the stars
came out. Benvolio lay there thinking that he preferred them to the Countess's wax candles. He went
back to town in a farmer's wagon, talking with the
honest rustic who drove it.

Very much in this way, when he had been on the
point of knocking at the gate of the Countess's heart

and asking ardently to be admitted, he had paused, stood frowning, and then turned short and rambled away into solitude. She never knew how near, two or three times, he had come. Two or three times she had accused him of being rude, and this was nothing but the backward swing of the pendulum. One day it seemed to her that he was altogether too vexatious, and she reproached herself with her good nature. She had made herself too cheap; such conduct was beneath her dignity; she would take another tone. She closed her door to him, and bade her people say, whenever he came, that she was engaged. At first Benvolio only wondered. Oddly enough, he was not what is commonly called sensitive; he never supposed you meant to offend him; not being at all impertinent himself, he was not on the watch for impertinence in others. Only, when he fairly caught you in the act he was immensely disgusted. Therefore, as I say, he simply wondered what had suddenly made the Countess so busy; then he remembered certain other charming persons whom he knew, and went to see how the world wagged with them.· But they rendered the Countess eminent service; she gained by comparison, and Benvolio began to miss her. All that other charming women were who led the life of the world (as it is called) the Countess was in a superior, in a perfect degree; she was the ripest fruit of a high civilization; her companions and rivals, beside her, had but a pallid bloom, an acrid savour. Benvolio had a relish in all things for the best, and he found himself breathing sighs under the Countess's darkened windows. He wrote to her, asking why in the world she treated him so cruelly, and then she knew that her charm was working. She was careful not to answer his letter, and to see that he was refused at her gate as inexorably as ever. It is an ill wind that blows nobody good, and Benvolio, one night after his dismissal, wandered about the moonlit streets till nearly morning, composing the finest verses he had ever produced. The subscribers to the magazine to which he sent them were at least the gainers. But unlike many poets, Benvolio did not on this occasion bury his passion in his poem; or if he did, its ghost was stalking abroad the very next night. He went again to the Countess's gate, and again it was closed in his face. So, after a very moderate amount of hesitation, he bravely (and with a dexterity which surprised him), scaled her garden wall and

dropped down in the moonshine, upon her lawn. I
don't know whether she was expecting him, but if
she had been, the matter could not have been better
arranged. She was sitting in a little niche of shrubbery, with no protector but a microscopic lap-dog.
She pretended to be scandalised at his audacity, but
his audacity carried the hour. " This time certainly,"
thought the Countess, " he will make his declaration.
He didn't jump that wall, at the risk of his neck,
simply to ask me for a cup of tea." Not a bit of it;
Benvolio was devoted, but he was not more explict
than before. He declared that this was the happiest
hour of his life; that there was a charming air of
romance in his position; that, honestly, he thanked
the Countess for having made him desperate; that he
would never come to see her again but by the garden
wall; that something, to night—what was it?—was
vastly becoming to her; that he devoutly hoped she
would receive no one else; that his admiration for
her was unbounded; that the stars, finally, had a
curious pink light! He looked at her, through the
flower-scented dusk, with admiring eyes; but he
looked at the stars as well; he threw back his head
and folded his arms, and let the conversation flag

while he examined the firmament. He observed also the long shafts of light proceeding from the windows of the house, as they fell upon the lawn and played among the shrubbery. The Countess had always thought him a singular man, but to-night she thought him more singular than ever. She became satirical, and the point of her satire was that he was after all but a dull fellow; that his admiration was a poor compliment; that he would do well to turn his attention to astronomy! In answer to this he came perhaps (to the Countess's sense) as near as he had ever come to making a declaration.

"Dear lady," he said, "you don't begin to know how much I admire you!"

She left her place at this, and walked about her lawn, looking at him askance while he talked, trailing her embroidered robe over the grass and fingering the folded petals of her flowers. He made a sort of sentimental profession of faith; he assured her that she represented his ideal of a certain sort of woman. This last phrase made her pause a moment and stare at him wide-eyed. "Oh, I mean the finest sort," he cried—"the sort that exerts the widest sway! You represent the world and everything that the world can give, and you represent them at their best—in their most generous, most graceful, most inspiring form. If a man were a revolutionist, you would reconcile him to society. You are a divine embodiment of all the amenities, the refinements, the complexities of life! You are the flower of urbanity, of culture, of tradition! You are the product of so many influences that it widens one's horizon to know you; of you too it is true that to admire you is a liberal education! Your charm is irresistible; I assure you I don't resist it!"

Compliments agreed with the Countess, as we may say; they not only made her happier, but they made her better. It became a matter of conscience with her to deserve them. These were magnificent ones, and she was by no means indifferent to them. Her cheek faintly flushed, her eyes vaguely glowed, and though her beauty, in the literal sense, was questionable, all that Benvolio said of her had never seemed more true. He said more in the same strain, and she listened without interrupting him. But at last she suddenly became impatient; it seemed to her that this was after all a tolerably inexpensive sort of wooing. But she did not betray her impatience

with any petulance; she simply shook her finger a
moment, to enjoin silence, and then she said, in a
voice of extreme gentleness—"You have too much
imagination!" He answered that, to do her perfect
justice, he had too little. To this she replied that it
was not of her any longer he was talking; he had
left her far behind. He was spinning fancies about
some highly subtilized figment of his brain. The
best answer to this, it seemed to Benvolio, was to
seize her hand and kiss it. I don't know what the
Countess thought of this form of argument; I in-
cline to think it both pleased and vexed her; it was
at once too much and too little. She snatched her
hand away and went rapidly into the house. Although Benvolio immediately followed her, he was
unable to overtake her; she had retired into impenetrable seclusion. A short time afterwards she left
town and went for the summer to an estate which
she possessed in a distant part of the country.

III

BENVOLIO was extremely fond of the country, but he remained in town after all his friends had departed. Many of them made him promise that he would come and see them. He promised, or half promised, but when he reflected that in almost every case he would find a house full of fellow-guests, to whose pursuits he would have to conform, and that if he rambled away with a valued duodecimo in his pocket to spend the morning alone in the woods, he would be denounced as a marplot and a selfish brute, he felt no great desire to pay visits. He had, as we know, his moods of expansion and of contraction ; he had been tolerably inflated for many months past, and now he had begun to take in sail. And then I suspect the foolish fellow had no money to travel withal. He had lately put all his available funds into the purchase of a picture—an estimable work

of the Venetian school, which had been suddenly
thrown into the market. It was offered for a
moderate sum, and Benvolio, who was one of the
first to see it, secured it, and hung it triumphantly
in his room. It had all the classic Venetian glow,
and he used to lie on his divan by the hour, gazing
at it. It had, indeed, a peculiar property, of which
I have known no other example. Most pictures that
are remarkable for their colour (especially if they
have been painted for a couple of centuries), need a
flood of sunshine on the canvas to bring it out. But
this remarkable work seemed to have a hidden radi-
ance of its own, which showed brightest when the
room was half darkened. When Benvolio wished
especially to enjoy his treasure he dropped his Venetian blinds, and the picture bloomed out into the cool
dusk with enchanting effect. It represented, in a fantastic way, the story of Perseus and Andromeda—
the beautiful naked maiden chained to a rock, on
which, with picturesque incongruity, a wild fig-tree
was growing; the green Adriatic tumbling at her
feet, and a splendid brown-limbed youth in a curious
helmet hovering near her on, a winged horse. The
journey his fancy made as he lay and looked at his

picture Benvolio preferred to any journey he might make by the public conveyances.

But he resorted for entertainment, as he had often done before, to the windows overlooking the old garden behind his house. As the summer deepened, of course the charm of the garden increased. It grew more tangled and bosky and mossy, and sent forth sweeter and heavier odours into the neighbouring air. It was a perfect solitude ; Benvolio had never seen a visitor there. One day, therefore, at this time, it puzzled him most agreeably to perceive a young girl sitting under one of the trees. She sat there a long time, and though she was at a distance, he managed, by looking long enough, to make out that she was pretty. She was dressed in black, and when she left her place her step had a kind of nun-like gentleness and demureness. Although she was alone, there was something timid and tentative in her movements. She wandered away and disappeared from sight, save that here and there he saw her white parasol gleaming in the gaps of the foliage. Then she came back to her seat under the great tree, and remained there for some time, arranging in her lap certain flowers that she had gathered. Then she rose again and vanished,

and Benvolio waited in vain for her return.   She had
evidently gone into the house.   The next day he saw
her again, and the next, and the next.   On these
occasions she had a book in her hand, and she sat in
her former place a long time, and read it with an air
of great attention.   Now and then she raised her head
and glanced toward the house, as if to keep something
in sight which divided her care ; and once or twice
she laid down her book and tripped away to her
hidden duties with a lighter step than she had shown
the first day.   Benvolio formed a theory that she had
an invalid parent, or a relation of some kind, who was
unable to walk, and had been moved into a window
overlooking the garden. She always took up her book
again when she came back, and bent her pretty head
over it with 'charming earnestness.   Benvolio had
already discovered that her head was pretty.   He
fancied it resembled a certain exquisite little head on
a Greek silver coin which lay, with several others, in
an agate cup on his table.   You see he had also already taken to fancying, and I offer this as the excuse
for his staring at his modest neighbour by the hour.
But he was not during these' hours idle, because he
was—I can't say falling in love with her ; he knew her

too little for that, and besides, he was in love with the Countess—but because he was at any rate cudgelling his brains about her. Who was she? what was she? why had he never seen her before? The house in which she apparently lived was in another street from Benvolios own, but he went out of his way on purpose to look at it. It was an ancient grizzled, sad-faced structure, with grated windows on the ground floor; it looked like a convent or a prison. Over a wall, beside it, there tumbled into the street some stray tendrils of a wild creeper from Benvolio's garden. Suddenly Benvolio began to suspect that the book the young girl in the garden was reading was none other than a volume of his own, put forth some six months before. His volume had a white cover and so had this; white covers are rather rare, and there was nothing impossible either in this young lady's reading his book or in her finding it interesting. Very many other women had done the same. Benvolio's neighbour had a pencil in her pocket, which she every now and then drew forth, to make with it a little mark on her page. This quiet gesture gave the young man an exquisite pleasure.

I am ashamed to say how much time he spent,

for a week, at his window. Every day the young
girl came into the garden. At last there occurred
a rainy day—a long, warm summer's rain—and she
staid within doors. He missed her quite acutely,
and wondered, half-smiling, half-frowning, that her
absence should make such a difference for him. He
actually depended upon her. He was ignorant of her
name ; he knew neither the colour of her eyes nor the
shade of her hair, nor the sound of her voice ; it was
very likely that if he were to meet her face to face,
elsewhere, he would not recognise her. But she
interested him ; he liked her ; he found her little
indefinite, black-dressed figure sympathetic. He
used to find the Countess sympathetic, and certainly
the Countess was as unlike this quiet garden-nymph
as she could very well be and be yet a charming
woman. Benvolio's sympathies, as we know, were
large. After the rain the young girl came out
again, and now she had another book, having apparently finished Benvolio's. He was gratified to
observe that she bestowed upon this one a much
more wandering attention. Sometimes she let it
drop listlessly at her side, and seemed to lose herself in maidenly reverie. Was she thinking how

much more beautiful Benvolio's verses were than others of the day? Was she perhaps repeating them to herself? It charmed Benvolio to suppose she might be; for he was not spoiled in this respect. The Countess knew none of his poetry by heart; she was nothing of a reader. She had his book on her table, but he once noticed that half the leaves were uncut.

After a couple of days of sunshine the rain came back again, to our hero's infinite annoyance, and this time it lasted several days. The garden lay dripping and desolate; its charm had quite departed. These days passed gloomily for Benvolio; he decided that rainy weather, in summer, in town, was intolerable. He began to think of the Countess again—he was sure that over her broad lands the summer sun was shining. He saw them, in envious fancy, studded with joyous Watteau-groups, feasting and making music under the shade of ancestral beeches. What a charming life! he thought—what brilliant, enchanted, memorable days! He had said the very reverse of all this, as you remember, three weeks before. I don't know that he had ever devoted a formula to the idea that men of imagination are not bound to be consistent, but he certainly conformed to its spirit. We are not, however, by any means at the end of his inconsistencies. He immediately wrote a letter to the Countess, asking her if he might pay her a visit.

Shortly after he had sent his letter the weather mended, and he went out for a walk. The sun was near setting; the streets were all ruddy and golden with its light, and the scattered rain-clouds, broken into a thousand little particles, were flecking the sky like a shower of opals and amethysts. Benvolio stopped, as he sauntered along, to gossip a while with his friend the bookseller. The bookseller was a foreigner and a man of taste; his shop was in the arcade of the great square. When Benvolio went in he was serving a lady, and the lady was dressed in black. Benvolio just now found it natural to notice a lady who was dressed in black, and the fact that this lady's face was averted made observation at once more easy and more fruitless. But at last her errand was finished; she had been ordering several books, and the bookseller was writing down their names. Then she turned round, and Benvolio saw her face. He stood staring at her most inconsiderately, for he felt an immediate certainty that she was the bookish damsel of the garden. She gave a glance round the shop, at the books on the walls, at the prints and busts, the apparatus of learning, in various forms, that it contained, and then, with the soundless, half-furtive step which Benvolio now knew so well, she took her departure. Benvolio seized the startled bookseller by the two hands and besieged him with questions. The bookseller, however, was able to answer but few of them. The young girl had been in his shop but once before, and had simply left an address, without any name. It was the address of which Benvolio had assured himself. The books she had ordered were all learned works—disquisitions on philosophy, on history, on the natural sciences, matters, all of them, in which she seemed an expert. For some of the volumes that she had just bespoken the bookseller was to send to foreign countries; the others were to be despatched that evening to the address which the young girl had left. As Benvolio stood there the old bibliophile gathered these latter together, and while he was so engaged he uttered a little cry of distress : one of the volumes of a set was missing. The work was a rare one, and it would be

hard to repair the loss. Benvolio on the instant had
an inspiration ; he demanded leave of his friend to
act as messenger : he himself would carry the books,
as if he came from the shop, and he would explain
the absence of the lost volume, and the bookseller's
views about replacing it, far better than one of the
hirelings. He asked leave, I say, but he did not wait
till it was given ; he snatched up the pile of books
and strode triumphantly away !

IV

As there was no name on the parcel, Benvolio, on reaching the old gray house over the wall of whose court an adventurous tendril stretched its long arm into the street, found himself wondering in what terms he should ask to have speech of the person for whom the books were intended. At any hazard he was determined not to retreat until he had caught a glimpse of the interior and its inhabitants; for this was the same man, you must remember, who had scaled the moonlit wall of the Countess's garden. An old serving woman in a quaint cap answered his summons, and stood blinking out at the fading day-light from a little wrinkled white face, as if she had never been compelled to take so direct a look at it before. He informed her that he had come from the bookseller's, and that he had been charged with a personal message for the venerable gentleman who had bespoken the parcel. Might he crave license to speak with him? This obsequious phrase was an improvisation of the moment—he had shaped it on the chance. But Benvolio had an indefinable conviction that it would fit the case; the only thing that surprised him was the quiet complaisance of the old woman.

"If it's on a bookish errand you come, sir," she said, with a little wheezy sigh, "I suppose I only do my duty in admitting you!"

She led him into the house, through various dusky chambers, and at last ushered him into an apartment of which the side opposite to the door was occupied by a broad, low casement. Through its small old panes there came a green dim light—the light of the low western sun shining through the wet trees of the famous garden. Everything else was ancient and brown; the walls were covered with tiers upon tiers of books. Near the window, in the still twilight, sat two persons, one of whom rose as Benvolio came in. This was the young girl of the garden— the young girl who had been an hour since at the bookseller's. The other was an old man, who turned his head, but otherwise sat motionless.

Both his movement and his stillness immediately
announced to Benvolio's quick perception that he was
blind. In his quality of poet Benvolio was inventive ;
a brain that is constantly tapped for rhymes is tolerably alert. In a few moments, therefore, he had
given a vigorous push to the wheel of fortune.
Various things had happened. He had made a soft,
respectful speech, he hardly knew about what; and
the old man had told him he had a delectable voice
—a voice that seemed to belong rather to a person
of education than to a tradesman's porter. Benvolio
confessed to having picked up an education, and the
old man had thereupon bidden the young girl offer
him a seat. Benvolio chose his seat where he could
see her, as she sat at the low-browed casement. The
bookseller in the square thought it likely Benvolio
would come back that evening and give him an account of his errand, and before he closed his shop he
looked up and down the street, to see whether the
young man was approaching. Benvolio came, but
the shop was closed. This he never noticed, however ; he walked three times round all the arcades,
without noticing it. He was thinking of something
else. He had sat all the evening with the blind old

scholar and his daughter, and he was thinking intently, ardently of them. When I say of them, of
course I mean of the daughter.

A few days afterwards he got a note from the
Countess, saying it would give her pleasure to receive
his visit. He immediately wrote to her that, with a
thousand regrets, he found himself urgently occupied
in town and must beg leave to defer his departure for
a day or two. The regrets were perfectly sincere, but
the plea was none the less valid. Benvolio had become deeply interested in his tranquil neighbours,
and, for the moment, a certain way the young girl
had of looking at him—fixing her eyes, first, with a
little vague, half-absent smile, on an imaginary point
above his head, and then slowly dropping them till
they met his own—was quite sufficient to make him
happy. He had called once more on her father, and
once more, and yet once more, and he had a vivid
prevision that he should often call again. He had
been in the garden and found its mild mouldiness
even more delightful on a nearer view. He had
pulled off his very ill-fitting mask, and let his neighbours know that his trade was not to carry parcels,
but to scribble verses. The old man had never heard

of his verses ; he read nothing that had been published later than the sixth century ; and nowadays he could read only with his daughter's eyes. Benvolio had seen the little white volume on the table, and assured himself it was his own ; and he noted the fact that in spite of its well-thumbed air, the young girl had never given her father a hint of its contents. I said just now that several things had happened in the first half hour of Benvolio's first visit. One of them was that this modest maiden fell in love with our young man. What happened when she learned that he was the author of the little white volume, I hardly know how to express ; her innocent passion began to throb and flutter. Benvolio possessed an old quarto volume bound in Russia leather, about which there clung an agreeable pungent odour. In this old quarto he kept a sort of diary—if that can be called a diary in which a whole year had sometimes been allowed to pass without an entry. On the other hand, there were some interminable records of a single day. Turning it over you would have chanced, not infrequently, upon the name of the Countess; and at this time you would have observed on every page some mention of "the

Professor" and of a certain person named Scholastica.
Scholastica, you will immediately guess, was the Professor's daughter. Probably this was not her own
name, but it was the name by which Benvolio preferred to know her, and we need not be more exact
than he. By this time of course he knew a great
deal about her, and about her venerable sire. The
Professor, before the loss of his eyesight and his
health, had been one of the stateliest pillars of the
University. He was now an old man; he had married late in life. When his infirmities came upon
him he gave up his chair and his classes and buried
himself in his library. He made his daughter his
reader and his secretary, and his prodigious memory
assisted her clear young voice and her softly-moving
pen. He was held in great honour in the scholastic
world; learned men came from afar to consult the
blind sage and to appeal to his wisdom as to the
ultimate law. The University settled a pension upon
him, and he dwelt in a dusky corner, among the aca-
demic shades. The pension was small, but the old
scholar and the young girl lived with conventual
simplicity. It so happened, however, that he had a
brother, or rather a half-brother, who was not a

bookish man, save as regarded his ledger and day-
book. This personage had made money in trade,
and had retired, wifeless and childless, into the old
gray house attached to Benvolio's garden. He had
the reputation of a skinflint, a curmudgeon, a blood-
less old miser who spent his days in shuffling about
his mouldy mansion, making his pockets jingle, and
his nights in lifting his money-bags out of trapdoors
and counting over his hoard. He was nothing but
a chilling shadow, an evil name, a pretext for a
curse ; no one had ever seen him, much less crossed
his threshold. But it seemed that he had a soft spot
in his heart. He wrote one day to his brother, whom
he had not seen for years, that the rumour had come
to him that he was blind, infirm, and poor ; that he
himself had a large house with a garden behind it ;
and that if the Professor were not too proud, he was
welcome to come and lodge there. The Professor
had come, in this way, a few weeks before, and
though it would seem that to a sightless old ascetic
all lodgings might be the same, he took a great
satisfaction in his new abode. His daughter found
it a paradise, compared with their two narrow chambers under the old gable of the University, where,

amid the constant coming and going of students,
a young girl was compelled to lead a cloistered
life.

Benvolio had assigned as his motive for intrusion,
when he had been obliged to acknowledge his real
character, an irresistible desire to ask the old man's
opinion on certain knotty points of philosophy.
This was a pardonable fiction, for the event, at any
rate, justified it.   Benvolio, when he was fairly
launched in a philosophical discussion, was capable
of forgetting that there was anything in the world
but metaphysics ; he revelled in transcendent ab-
stractions and became unconscious of all concrete
things—even of that most brilliant of concrete things,
the Countess.   He longed to embark on a voyage of
discovery on the great sea of pure reason.   He knew
that from such voyages the deep-browed adventurer
rarely returns ; but if he were to find an El Dorado
of thought, why should he regret the dusky world of
fact ?   Benvolio had high colloquies with the Professor, who was a devout Neo-Platonist, and whose
venerable wit had spun to subtler tenuity the ethereal
speculations of the Alexandrian school.   Benvolio
at this season declared that study and science were

the only game in life worth the candle, and wondered how he could ever for an instant have cared for more vulgar exercises. He turned off a little poem in the style of Milton's *Penseroso*, which, if it had not quite the merit of that famous effusion, was at least the young man's own happiest performance. When Benvolio liked a thing he liked it as a whole—it appealed to all his senses. He relished its accidents, its accessories, its material envelope. In the satisfaction he took in his visits to the Professor it would have been hard to say where the charm of philosophy began or ended. If it began with a glimpse of the old man's mild, sightless blue eyes, sitting fixed beneath his shaggy white brows like patches of pale winter sky under a high-piled cloud, it hardly ended before it reached the little black bow on Scholastica's slipper; and certainly it had taken a comprehensive sweep in the interval. There was nothing in his friends that had not a charm, an interest, a character, for his appreciative mind. Their seclusion, their stillness, their super-simple notions of the world and the world's ways, the faint, musty perfume of the University which hovered about them, their brown old apartment, impenetrable to the rumours of the town—all these things were part of his entertainment. Then the essence of it perhaps was that in this silent, simple life the intellectual key, if you touched it, was so finely resonant. In the way of thought there was nothing into which his friends were not initiated —nothing they could not understand. The mellow light of their low-browed room, streaked with the moted rays that slanted past the dusky book-shelves, was the atmosphere of intelligence. All this made them, humble folk as they were, not so simple as they at first appeared. They, too, in their own fashion, knew the world ; they were not people to be patronized ; to visit them was not a condescension, but a privilege.

In the Professor this was not surprising. He had passed fifty years in arduous study, and it was proper to his character and his office that he should be erudite and venerable. But his devoted little daughter seemed to Benvolio at first almost grotesquely wise. She was an anomaly, a prodigy, a charming monstrosity. Charming, at any rate, she was, and as pretty, I must lose no more time in saying, as had seemed likely to Benvolio at his window. And yet, even on a nearer view, her prettiness shone forth slowly. It was as if it had been covered with a series of film-like veils, which had to be successively drawn aside. And then it was such a homely, shrinking, subtle prettiness, that Benvolio, in the private record I have mentioned, never thought of calling it by the arrogant name of beauty. He called it by no name at all ; he contented himself with enjoying it—with looking into the young girl's mild gray eyes and saying things, on purpose, that caused her candid smile to deepen until (like the broadening ripple of a lake) it reached a particular dimple in her left cheek. This was its maximum ; no smile could do more, and Benvolio desired nothing better. Yet I cannot say he was in love with the young girl ; he only liked her. But he liked her, no doubt, as a man likes a thing but once in his life. As he knew her better, the oddity of her great learning quite faded away ; it seemed delightfully natural, and he only wondered why there were not more women of the same pattern. Scholastica had imbibed the wine of science instead of her mother's milk. Her mother had died in her infancy, leaving her cradled in an old folio, three-quarters opened, like a wide V. Her father had been her nurse, her playmate, her teacher, her life-long companion, her only friend. He taught her the Greek alphabet before she knew her own, and fed her with crumbs from his scholastic revels. She had taken submissively what was given her, and, without knowing it, she grew up a little handmaid of science.

Benvolio perceived that she was not in the least a woman of genius. The passion for knowledge, of its own motion, would never have carried her far. But she had a perfect understanding—a mind as clear and still and natural as a woodland pool, giving back an exact and definite image of everything that was presented to it. And then she was so teachable, so diligent, so indefatigable. Slender and meagre as she was, and rather pale too, with being much within doors, she was never tired, she never had a headache, she never closed her book or laid down a pen with a sigh. Benvolio said to himself that she was exquisitely constituted for helping a man. What a work he might do on summer mornings and winter nights, with that brightly demure little creature at his side, transcribing, recollecting, sympathising! He wondered how much she cared for these things herself; whether a woman could care for them without being

dry and harsh. It was in a great measure for information on this point that he used to question her
eyes with the frequency that I have mentioned.
But they never gave him a perfectly direct answer,
and this was why he came and came again. They
seemed to him to say, "If you could lead a student's
life for my sake, I could be a life-long household
scribe for yours." Was it divine philosophy that
made Scholastica charming, or was it she that made
philosophy divine? I cannot relate everything that
came to pass between these young people, and I
must leave a great deal to your imagination. The
summer waned, and when the autumn afternoons
began to grow vague, the quiet couple in the old
gray house had expanded to a talkative trio. For
Benvolio the days had passed very fast; the trio had
talked of so many things. He had spent many an
hour in the garden with the young girl, strolling in
the weedy paths, or resting on a moss-grown bench.
She was a delightful listener, because she not only
attended, but she followed. Benvolio had known
women to fix very beautiful eyes upon him, and
watch with an air of ecstasy the movement of his

lips, and yet had found them three minutes afterwards quite incapable of saying what he was talking
about. Scholastica gazed at him, but she understood
him too.

V.

YOU will say that my description of Benvolio has done him injustice, and that, far from being the sentimental weathercock I have depicted, he is proving himself a model of constancy. But mark the sequel! It was at this moment precisely, that, one morning, having gone to bed the night before singing pæans to divine philosophy, he woke up with a headache, and in the worst of humours with abstract science. He remembered Scholastica telling him that she never had headaches, and the memory quite annoyed him. He suddenly found himself thinking of her as a neat little mechanical toy, wound up to turn pages and write a pretty hand, but with neither a head nor a heart that was capable of human ailments. He fell asleep again, and in one of those brief but vivid dreams that sometimes occur in the morning hours, he had a brilliant vision

of the Countess. *She* was human beyond a doubt,
and duly familiar with headaches and heartaches.
He felt an irresistible desire to see her and to tell
her that he adored her. This satisfaction was not
unattainable, and before the day was over he was
well on his way toward enjoying it. He left town
and made his pilgrimage to her estate, where he
found her holding her usual court and leading a
merry life. He had meant to stay with her a week;
he staid two months—the most entertaining months
he had ever known. I cannot pretend of course
to enumerate the diversions of this fortunate circle,
or to say just how Benvolio spent every hour of
his time. But if the summer had passed quickly
with him, the autumn moved with a tread as light.
He thought once in a while of Scholastica and her
father—once in a while, I say, when present occupations suffered his thoughts to wander. This was
not often, for the Countess had always, as the phrase
is, a hundred arrows in her quiver.. You see, the
negative, with Benvolio, always implied as distinct
a positive, and his excuse for being inconstant on
one side was that he was at such a time very as-
siduous on another. He developed at this period a

talent as yet untried and unsuspected; he proved himself capable of writing brilliant dramatic poetry. The long autumn evenings, in a great country house, were a natural occasion for the much-abused pastime known as private theatricals. The Countess had a theatre, and abundant material for a troupe of amateur players; all that was lacking was a play exactly adapted to her resources. She proposed to Benvolio to write one; the idea took his fancy; he shut himself up in the library, and in a week produced a masterpiece. He had found the subject, one day when he was pulling over the Countess's books, in an old MS. chronicle written by the chaplain of one of her late husband's ancestors. It was the germ of an admirable drama, and Benvolio greatly enjoyed his attempt to make a work of art of it. All his genius, all his imagination went into it. This was the proper mission of his faculties, he cried to himself—the study of warm human passions, the painting of rich dramatic pictures, not the dry chopping of logic. His play was acted with brilliant success, the Countess herself representing the heroine. Benvolio had never seen her don the buskin, and had no idea of her aptitude

for the stage; but she was inimitable, she was a
natural artist. What gives charm to life, Benvolio
hereupon said to himself, is the element of the
unexpected ; and this one finds only in women of
the Countess's type. And I should do wrong to
imply that he here made an invidious comparison,
for he did not even think of Scholastica. His play
was repeated several times, and people were invited
to see it from all the country round. There was
a great bivouac of servants in the castle-court ; in
the cold November nights a bonfire was lighted to
keep the servants warm. It was a great triumph
for Benvolio, and he frankly enjoyed it. He knew
he enjoyed it, and how great a triumph it was, and
he felt every disposition to drain the cup to the
last drop. He relished his own elation, and found
himself excellent company. He began immediately
another drama—a comedy this time—and he was
greatly interested to observe that when his work
was on the stocks he found himself regarding all
the people about him as types and available figures.
Everything he saw or heard was grist to his mill;
everything presented itself as possible material.
Life on these terms became really very interesting,

and for several nights the laurels of Molière kept Benvolio awake.

Delightful as this was, however, it could not last for ever. When the winter nights had begun, the Countess returned to town, and Benvolio came back with her, his unfinished comedy in his pocket. During much of the journey he was silent and abstracted, and the Countess supposed he was thinking of how he should make the most of that capital situation in his third act. The Countess's perspicacity was just sufficient to carry her so far—to lead her, in other words, into plausible mistakes. Benvolio was really wondering what in the name of mystery had suddenly become of his inspiration, and why the witticisms in his play and his comedy had begun to seem as mechanical as the cracking of the post-boy's whip. He looked out at the scrubby fields, the rusty woods, the sullen sky, and asked himself whether *that* was the world to which it had been but yesterday his high ambition to hold up the mirror. The Countess's *dame de compagnie* sat opposite to him in the carriage. Yesterday he thought her, with her pale, discreet face, and her eager movements that pretended to be

indifferent, a finished specimen of an entertaining
genus. To-day he could only say that if there
was a whole genus it was a thousand pities, for
the poor lady struck him as miserably false and
servile. The real seemed hideous; he felt home-
sick for his dear familiar rooms between the garden
and the square, and he longed to get into them
and bolt his door and bury himself in his old
arm-chair and cultivate idealism for evermore. The
first thing he actually did on getting into them
was to go to the window and look out into the
garden. It had greatly changed in his absence,
and the old maimed statues, which all the summer had
been comfortably muffled in verdure, were now, by
an odd contradiction of propriety, standing white
and naked in the cold. I don't exactly know how
soon it was that Benvolio went back to see his
neighbours. It was after no great interval, and
yet it was not immediately. He had a bad
conscience, and he was wondering what he should
say to them. It seemed to him now (though he
had not thought of it sooner), that they might accuse him of neglecting them. He had appealed
to their friendship, he had professed the highest

esteem for them, and then he had turned his back on them without farewell, and without a word of explanation. He had not written to them; in truth during his sojourn with the Countess, it would not have been hard for him to persuade himself that they were people he had only dreamed about, or read about, at most, in some old volume of memoirs. People of their value, he could now imagine them saying, were not to be taken up and dropped for a fancy; and if friendship was not to be friendship as they themselves understood it, it was better that he should forget them at once and for ever. It is perhaps too much to affirm that he imagined them saying all this ; they were too mild and civil, too unused to acting in self-defence. But they might easily receive him in a way that would imply a delicate resentment. Benvolio felt profaned, dishonoured, almost contaminated ; so that perhaps when he did at last return to his friends, it was because that was the simplest way to be purified. How did they receive him ? I told you a good way back that Scholastica was in love with him, and you may arrange the scene in any manner that best accords with this circum-

stance. Her forgiveness, of course, when once
that chord was touched, was proportionate to her
displeasure. But Benvolio took refuge both from
his own compunction and from the young girl's
reproaches, in whatever form these were conveyed,
in making a full confession of what he was pleased
to call his frivolity. As he walked through the
naked garden with Scholastica, kicking the wrinkled
leaves, he told her the whole story of his sojourn
with the Countess. The young girl listened with
bright intentness, as she would have listened to some
thrilling passage in a romance; but she neither
sighed, nor looked wistful, nor seemed to envy the
Countess or to repine at her own ignorance of the
great world. It was all too remote for comparison;
it was not, for Scholastica, among the things that
might have been. Benvolio talked to her very freely
about the Countess. If she liked it, he found on
his side that it eased his mind; and as he said
nothing that the Countess would not have been
flattered by, there was no harm done. Although,
however, Benvolio uttered nothing but praise of
this distinguished lady, he was very frank in saying
that she and her way of life always left him at

the end in a worse humour than when they found him. They were very well in their way, he said, but their way was not his way—it only seemed so at moments. For him, he was convinced, the only real felicity was in the pleasures of study! Scholastica answered that it gave her high satisfaction to hear this, for it was her father's belief that Benvolio had a great aptitude for philosophical research, and that it was a sacred duty to cultivate so rare a faculty.

"And what is your belief?" Benvolio asked, remembering that the young girl knew several of his poems by heart.

Her answer was very simple. "I believe you are a poet."

"And a poet oughtn't to run the risk of turning pedant?"

"No," she answered; "a poet ought to run all risks —even that one which for a poet is perhaps most cruel. But he ought to escape them all!"

Benvolio took great satisfaction in hearing that the Professor deemed that he had in him the making of a philosopher, and it gave an impetus to the zeal with which he returned to work.

VI

OF course even the most zealous student cannot work always, and often, after a very philosophic day, Benvolio spent with the Countess a very sentimental evening. It is my duty as a veracious historian not to conceal the fact that he discoursed to the Countess about Scholastica. He gave such a puzzling description of her that the Countess declared that she must be a delightfully quaint creature and that it would be vastly amusing to know her. She hardly supposed Benvolio was in love with this little bookworm in petticoats, but to make sure—if that might be called making sure—she deliberately asked him. He said No; he hardly saw how he could be, since he was in love with the Countess herself! For a while this answer satisfied her, but as the winter went by she began to wonder whether there were not such a thing as a man being in love with two

women at once. During many months that followed,
Benvolio led a kind of double life. Sometimes it
charmed him and gave him an inspiring sense of
personal power. He haunted the domicile of his
gentle neighbours, and drank deep of the garnered
wisdom of the ages ; and he made appearances as
frequent in the Countess's drawing-room, where he
played his part with magnificent zest and ardour.
It was a life of alternation and contrast, and it
really demanded a vigorous and elastic temperament.
Sometimes his own seemed to him quite inadequate
to the occasion—he felt fevered, bewildered, exhausted.
But when it came to the point of choosing one thing
or the other, it was impossible to give up either his
worldly habits or his studious aspirations. Benvolio
raged inwardly at the cruel limitations of the human
mind, and declared it was a great outrage that a
man should not be personally able to do everything
he could imagine doing. I hardly know how she
contrived it, but the Countess was at this time a
more engaging woman than she had ever been. Her
beauty acquired an ampler and richer cast, and she
had a manner of looking at you as she slowly turned
away with a vague reproachfulness that was at the

same time an encouragement, which had lighted a hopeless flame in many a youthful breast. Benvolio one day felt in the mood for finishing his comedy, and the Countess and her friends acted it. Its success was no less brilliant than that of its predecessor, and the manager of the theatre immediately demanded the privilege of producing it. You will hardly believe me, however, when I tell you that on the night that his comedy was introduced to the public, its eccentric author sat discussing the absolute and the relative with the Professor and his daughter. Benvolio had all winter been observing that Scholastica never looked so pretty as when she sat, of a winter's night, plying a quiet needle in the mellow circle of a certain antique brass lamp. On the night in question he happened to fall a-thinking of this picture, and he tramped out across the snow for the express purpose of looking at it. It was sweeter even than his memory promised, and it banished every thought of his theatrical honours from his head. Scholastica gave him some tea, and her tea, for mysterious reasons, was delicious ; better, strange to say, than that of the Countess, who, however, it must be added, recovered her ground in coffee. The Professor's parsimonious brother owned

a ship which made voyages to China and brought
him goodly chests of the incomparable plant. He
sold the cargo for great sums, but he kept a chest
for himself. It was always the best one, and he had
at this time carefully measured out a part of his
annual dole, made it into a little parcel, and presented it to Scholastica. This is the secret history
of Benvolio's fragrant cups. While he was drinking
them on the night I speak of—I am ashamed to say
how many he drank—his name, at the theatre, was
being tossed across the footlights to a brilliant,
clamorous multitude, who hailed him as the redeemer
of the national stage. But I am not sure that he
even told his friends that his play was being acted.
Indeed, this was hardly possible, for I meant to say
just now that he had forgotten it.

It is very certain, however, that he enjoyed the
criticisms the next day in the newspapers. Radiant
and jubilant, he went to see the Countess, with half
a dozen of them in his pocket. He found her looking
terribly dark. She had been at the theatre, prepared
to revel in his triumph—to place on his head with her
own hand, as it were, the laurel awarded by the
public ; and his absence had seemed to her a sort of

personal slight. Yet his triumph had nevertheless
given her an exceeding pleasure, for it had been the
seal of her secret hopes of him. Decidedly he was
to be a great man, and this was not the moment
for letting him go! At the same time there was
something noble in his indifference, his want oi
eagerness, his finding it so easy to forget his honours.
It was only an intellectual Crœsus, the Countess said
to herself, who could afford to keep so loose an
account with fame. But she insisted on knowing
where he had been, and he told her he had beer
discussing philosophy and tea with the Professor.

"And was not the daughter there?" the Countess
demanded.

"Most sensibly!" he cried. And then he added
in a moment—"I don't know whether I ever told
you, but she's almost as pretty as you."

The Countess resented the compliment to Scholastica much more than she enjoyed the compliment to
herself. She felt an extreme curiosity to see this
inky-fingered syren, and as she seldom failed, sooner
or later, to compass her desires, she succeeded at last
in catching a glimpse of her innocent rival. To do
so she was obliged to set a great deal of machinery

in motion. She induced Benvolio to give a lunch, in his rooms, to some ladies who professed a desire to see his works of art, and of whom she constituted herself the chaperon. She took care that he threw open a certain vestibule that looked into the garden, and here, at the window, she spent much of her time. There was but a chance that Scholastica would come forth into the garden, but it was a chance worth staking something upon. The Countess gave to it time and temper, and she was finally rewarded. Scholastica came out. The poor girl strolled about for half an hour, in profound unconsciousness that the Countess's fine eyes were devouring her. The impression she made was singular. The Countess found her both pretty and ugly : she did not admire her herself, but she understood that Benvolio might. For herself, personally, she detested her, and when Scholastica went in and she turned away from the window, her first movement was to pass before a mirror, which showed her something that, impartially considered, seemed to her a thousand times more beautiful. The Countess made no comments, and took good care Benvolio did not suspect the trick she had played him. There was something more she

promised herself to do, and she impatiently awaited
her opportunity.

In the middle of the winter she announced to him
that she was going to spend ten days in the country;
she had received the most attractive accounts of the
state of things on her domain.   There had been great
snow-falls, and the sleighing was magnificent; the
lakes and streams were solidly frozen, there was an
unclouded moon, and the resident gentry were
skating, half the night, by torch-light.   The Countess
was passionately fond both of sleighing and skating,
and she found this picture irresistible.   And then she
was charitable, and observed that it would be a
kindness to the poor resident gentry, whose usual
pleasures were of a frugal sort, to throw open her
house and give a ball or two, with the village fiddlers.
Perhaps even they might organize a bear-hunt—an
entertainment at which, if properly conducted, a lady
might be present as spectator.   The Countess told
Benvolio all this one day as he sat with her in her
boudoir, in the fire-light, during the hour that pre-
cedes dinner.   She had said more than once that he
must decamp—that she must go and dress; but
neither of them had moved.   She did not invite him

to go with her to the country; she only watched him as he sat gazing with a frown at the fire-light—the crackling blaze of the great logs which had been cut in the Countess's bear-haunted forests. At last she rose impatiently, and fairly turned him out. After he had gone she stood for a moment looking at the fire, with the tip of her foot on the fender. She had not to wait long; he came back within the minute— came back and begged her leave to go with her to the country—to skate with her in the crystal moonlight and dance with her to the sound of the village violins. It hardly matters in what terms his request was granted ; the notable point is that he made it. He was her only companion, and when they were established in the castle the hospitality extended to the resident gentry was less abundant than had been promised. Benvolio, however, did not complain of the absence of it, because, for the week or so, he was passionately in love with his hostess. They took long sleigh-rides and drank deep of the poetry of winter. The blue shadows on the snow, the cold amber lights in the west, the leafless twigs against the snow-charged sky, all gave them ex- traordinary pleasure. The nights were even better, when the great silver stars, before the moonrise, glittered on the polished ice, and the young Countess and her lover, firmly joining hands, launched themselves into motion and into the darkness and went skimming for miles with their winged steps. On their return, before the great chimney-place in the old library, they lingered a while and drank little cups of wine heated with spices. It was perhaps here, cup in hand—this point is uncertain—that Benvolio broke through the last bond of his reserve, and told the Countess that he loved her, in a manner to satisfy her. To be his in all solemnity, his only and his for ever—this he explicitly, passionately, imperiously demanded.of her. After this she gave her ball to her country neighbours, and Benvolio danced, to a boisterous, swinging measure, with a dozen ruddy beauties dressed in the fashions of the year before last. The Countess danced with the lusty male counterparts of these damsels, but she found plenty of chances to watch Benvolio. Toward the end of the evening she saw him looking grave and bored, with very much such a frown in his forehead as when he had sat staring at the fire that last day in her boudoir. She said to herself for the hundredth time that he was the strangest of mortals.

On their return to the city she had frequent occasions to say it again. He looked at moments as if he had repented of his bargain—as if it did not at all suit him that his being the Countess's only lover should involve her being his only mistress. She deemed now that she had acquired the right to make him give an account of his time, and he did not conceal the fact that the first thing he had done on reaching town was to go to see his eccentric neighbours. She treated him hereupon to a passionate outburst of jealousy; called Scholastica a dozen harsh names—a little dingy blue-stocking, a little underhand, hypocritical Puritan; demanded he should promise never to speak to her again, and summoned him to make a choice once for all. Would he belong to her, or to that odious little school-mistress? It must be one thing or the other; he must take her or leave her; it was impossible she should have a lover who was so little to be depended upon. The Countess did not say this made her unhappy, but she repeated a dozen times that it made her ridiculous. Benvolio turned very pale;

she had never seen him so before ; a great struggle
was evidently taking place within him. A terrible
scene was the consequence. He broke out into
reproaches and imprecations ; he accused the
Countess of being his bad angel, of making him
neglect his best faculties, mutilate his genius,
squander his life; and yet he confessed that he was
committed to her, that she fascinated him beyond
resistance, and that, at any sacrifice, he must still be
her slave. This confession gave the Countess un-
common satisfaction, and made up in a measure for
the unflattering remarks that accompanied it. She
on her side confessed—what she had always been too
proud to acknowledge hitherto—that she cared vastly
for him, and that she had waited for long months for
him to say something of this kind. They parted on
terms which it would be hard to define—full of
mutual resentment and devotion, at once adoring and
hating each other. All this was deep and stirring
emotion, and Benvolio, as an artist, always in one
way or another found his profit in emotion, even
when it lacerated or suffocated him. There was,
moreover, a sort of elation in having burnt his ships
behind him, and vowed to seek his fortune, his

intellectual fortune, in the tumult of life and action. He did no work; his power of work, for the time at least, was paralyzed. Sometimes this frightened him; it seemed as if his genius were dead, his career cut short; at other moments his faith soared supreme; he heard, in broken murmurs, the voice of the muse, and said to himself that he was only resting, waiting, storing up knowledge. Before long he felt tolerably tranquil again; ideas began to come to him, and the world to seem entertaining. He demanded of the Countess that, without further delay, their union should be solemnized. But the Countess, at that interview I have just related, had, in spite of her high spirit, received a great fright. Benvolio, stalking up and down with clenched hands and angry eyes, had seemed to her a terrible man to marry; and though she was conscious of a strong will of her own, as well as of robust nerves, she had shuddered at the thought that such scenes might often occur. She had hitherto seen little but the mild and genial, or at most the joyous and fantastic side of her friend's disposition; but it now appeared that there was another side to be taken into account, and that if

Benvolio had talked of sacrifices, these were not all
to be made by him. They say the world likes its
master—that a horse of high spirit likes being well
ridden. This may be true in the long run ; but the
Countess, who was essentially a woman of the world,
was not yet prepared to pay our young man the
tribute of her luxurious liberty. She admired him
more, now that she was afraid of him, but at the same
time she liked him a trifle less. She answered that
marriage was a very serious matter ; that they had
lately had a taste of each other's tempers ; that they
had better wait a while longer ; that she had made
up her mind to travel for a year, and that she strongly
recommended him to come with her, for travelling
was notoriously an excellent test of friendship.

VII.

SHE went to Italy, and Benvolio went with her; but before he went he paid a visit to his other mistress. He flattered himself that he had burned his ships behind him, but the fire was still visibly smouldering. It is true, nevertheless, that he passed a very strange half-hour with Scholastica and her father. The young girl had greatly changed; she barely greeted him; she looked at him coldly. He had no idea her face could wear that look; it vexed him to find it there. He had not been to see her for many weeks, and he now came to tell her that he was going away for a year; it is true these were not conciliatory facts. But she had taught him to think that she possessed in perfection the art of trustful resignation, of unprotesting, cheerful patience—virtues that sat so gracefully on her bended brow that the thought of their being at any rate supremely becoming took the edge from his remorse at making them necessary. But now Scholastica looked older as well as sadder, and decidedly not so pretty. Her figure was meagre, her movements were angular, her charming eye was dull. After the first minute he avoided this charming eye; it made him uncomfortable. Her voice she scarcely allowed him to hear. The Professor, as usual, was serene and frigid, impartial and transcendental. There was a chill in the air, a shadow between them. Benvolio went so far as to wonder that he had ever found a great attraction in the young girl, and his present disillusionment gave him even more anger than pain. He took leave abruptly and coldly, and puzzled his brain for a long time afterward over the mystery of Scholastica's reserve.

The Countess had said that travelling was a test of friendship; in this case friendship (or whatever the passion was to be called) promised for some time to resist the test. Benvolio passed six months of the liveliest felicity. The world has nothing better to offer to a man of sensibility than a first visit to Italy during those years of life when perception is at its keenest, when knowledge has arrived, and yet youth has not departed. He made with the Countess a long, slow progress through the lovely land, from the Alps to the Sicilian sea; and it seemed to him that his imagination, his intellect, his genius, expanded with every breath and rejoiced in every glance. The Countess was in an almost equal ecstasy, and their sympathy was perfect in all points save the lady's somewhat indiscriminate predilection for assemblies and receptions. She had a thousand letters of introduction to deliver, which entailed a vast deal of social exertion. Often, on balmy nights when he would have preferred to meditate among the ruins of the Forum, or to listen to the moonlit ripple of the Adriatic, Benvolio found himself dragged away to kiss the hand of a decayed princess, or to take a pinch from the snuff-box of an epicurean cardinal. But the cardinals, the princesses, the ruins, the warm southern tides which seemed the voice of history itself—these and a thousand other things resolved themselves into an immense pictorial spectacle—the very stuff that inspiration is made of. Everything Benvolio had written before coming to Italy now appeared to him worthless; this was the needful stamp, the consecration of talent. One day, however, his felicity was clouded; by a trifle you will

say, possibly; but you must remember that in men
of Benvolio's disposition primary impulses are almost
always produced by small accidents. The Countess,
speaking of the tone of voice of some one they had
met, happened to say that it reminded her of the
voice of that queer little woman at home—the
daughter of the blind professor. Was this pure
inadvertence, or was it malicious design? Benvolio
never knew, though he immediately demanded of
her, in surprise, when and where she had heard Scholastica's voice. His whole attention was aroused;
the Countess perceived it, and for a moment she
hesitated. Then she bravely replied that she had
seen the young girl in the musty old book-room
where she spent her dreary life. At these words,
uttered in a profoundly mocking tone, Benvolio had
an extraordinary sensation. He was walking with the
Countess in the garden of a palace, and they had
just approached the low balustrade of a terrace which
commanded a magnificent view. On one side were
violet Apennines, dotted here and there with a
gleaming castle or convent; on the other stood the
great palace through whose galleries the two had
just been strolling, with its walls incrusted with

medallions and its cornice charged with statues. But Benvolio's heart began to beat; the tears sprang to his eyes; the perfect landscape around him faded away and turned to blankness, and there rose before him, distinctly, vividly present, the old brown room that looked into the dull northern garden, tenanted by the quiet figures he had once told himself that he loved. He had a choking sensation and a sudden overwhelming desire to return to his own country.

The Countess would say nothing more than that the fancy had taken her one day to go and see Scholastica. " I suppose I may go where I please ! " she cried in the tone of the great lady who is accustomed to believe that her glance confers honour wherever it falls. " I am sure I did her no harm. She's a good little creature, and it's not her fault if she's so ridiculously plain." Benvolio looked at her intently, but he saw that he should learn nothing from her that she did not choose to tell. As he stood there he was amazed to find how natural, or at least how easy, it was to disbelieve her. She had been with the young girl; that accounted for anything; it accounted abundantly for Scholastica's painful constraint. What had the Countess said

and done? what infernal trick had she played upon
the poor girl's simplicity? He helplessly wondered,
but he felt that she could be trusted to hit her mark.
She had done him the honour to be jealous, and
in order to alienate Scholastica she had invented
some ingenious calumny against himself. He felt
sick and angry, and for a week he treated his companion with grim indifference. The charm was
broken, the cup of pleasure was drained. This
remained no secret to the Countess, who was furious
at the mistake she had made. At last she abruptly
told Benvolio that the test had failed; they must
separate; he would gratify her by taking his leave.
He asked no second permission, but bade her farewell in the midst of her little retinue, and went
journeying out of Italy with no other company than
his thick-swarming memories and projects.

The first thing he did on reaching home was to
repair to the Professor's abode. The old man's chair,
for the first time, was empty, and Scholastica was not
in the room. He went out into the garden, where,
after wandering hither and thither, he found the young
girl seated in a dusky arbour. She was dressed, as
usual, in black; but her head was drooping, her

empty hands were folded, and her sweet face was
more joyless even than when he had last seen it.
If she had been changed then, she was doubly
changed now. Benvolio looked round, and as the
Professor was nowhere visible, he immediately guessed
the cause of her mourning aspect. The good old
man had gone to join his immortal brothers, the
classic sages, and Scholastica was utterly alone.
She seemed frightened at seeing him, but he took
her hand, and she let him sit down beside her.
"Whatever you were once told that made you think
ill of me is detestably false," he said. "I have the
tenderest friendship for you, and now more than ever
I should like to show it." She slowly gathered courage
to meet his eyes; she found them reassuring, and at
last, though she never told him in what way her mind
had been poisoned, she suffered him to believe that
her old confidence had come back. She told him
how her father had died, and how, in spite of the
philosophic maxims he had bequeathed to her for her
consolation, she felt very lonely and helpless. Her
uncle had offered her a maintenance, meagre but
sufficient; she had the old serving-woman to keep
her company, and she meant to live in her present

abode and occupy herself with collecting her father's papers and giving them to the world according to a plan for which he had left particular directions. She seemed irresistibly tender and touching, and yet full of dignity and self-support. Benvolio fell in love with her again on the spot, and only abstained from telling her so because he remembered just in time that he had an engagement to be married to the Countess, and that this understanding had not yet been formally rescinded. He paid Scholastica a long visit, and they went in together and rummaged over her father's books and papers. The old scholar's literary memoranda proved to be extremely valuable ; it would be a useful and interesting task to give them to the world. When Scholastica heard Benvolio's high estimate 'of them her cheek began to glow and her spirit to revive. The present then was secure, she seemed to say to herself, and she would have occupation for many a month. He offered to give her every assistance in his power, and in con-sequence he came daily to see her. Scholastica lived so much out of the world that she was not obliged to trouble herself about vulgar gossip. Whatever jests were aimed at the young man for his visible

devotion to a mysterious charmer, he was very sure
that her ear was never wounded by base insinuations.
The old serving-woman sat in a corner, nodding over
her distaff, and the two friends held long confabulations
over yellow manuscripts in which the commentary,
it must be confessed, did not always adhere very
closely to the text. Six months elapsed, and Benvolio found an ineffable charm in this mild mixture
of sentiment and study. He had never in his life
been so long of the same mind; it really seemed
as if, as the phrase is, the fold were taken for ever—
as if he had done with the world and were ready to
live henceforth in the closet. He hardly thought of
the Countess, and they had no correspondence. She
was in Italy, in Greece, in the East, in the Holy Land,
in places and situations that taxed the imagination.

One day, in the darkness of the vestibule, after
he had left Scholastica, he was arrested by a little
old man of sordid aspect, of whom he could make
out hardly more than a pair of sharply-glowing eyes
and an immense bald head, polished like a ball of
ivory. He was a quite terrible little figure in his
way, and Benvolio at first was frightened. "Mr.
Poet," said the old man, "let me say a single word.

I give my niece a maintenance. She may do what she likes. But she forfeits every penny of her allowance and her expectations if she is fool enough to marry a fellow who scribbles rhymes. I am told they are sometimes an hour finding two that will match! Good evening, Mr. Poet!" Benvolio heard a sound like the faint jingle of loose coin in a breeches pocket, and the old man abruptly retreated into his domiciliary gloom. Benvolio had never seen him before, and he had no wish ever to see him again. He had not proposed to himself to marry Scholastica, and even if he had, I am pretty sure he would now have taken the modest view of the matter and decided that his hand and heart were an insufficient compensation for the relinquishment of a miser's fortune. The young girl never spoke of her uncle; he lived quite alone, apparently, haunting his upper chambers like a restless ghost, and sending her, by the old serving-woman, her slender monthly allowance, wrapped up in a piece of old newspaper. It was shortly after this that the Countess at last came back. Benvolio had been taking one of those long walks to which he had always been addicted, and passing through the public gardens on his way home,

he had sat down on a bench to rest. In a few moments
a carriage came rolling by; in it sat the Countess—
beautiful, sombre, solitary. He rose with a cere-
monious salute, and she went her way. But in five
minutes she passed back again, and this time her
carriage stopped. She gave him a single glance,
and he got in. For a week afterward Scholastica
vainly awaited him. What had happened? It had
happened that though she had proved herself both
false and cruel, the Countess again asserted her charm,
and our precious hero again succumbed to it. But
he resumed his visits to Scholastica after an interval
of neglect not long enough to be unpardonable;
the only difference was that now they were not so
frequent.

My story draws to a close, for I am afraid you
have already lost patience with the history of this
amiable weathercock. Another year ran its course,
and the Professor's manuscripts were arranged in
great piles and almost ready for the printer.
Benvolio had had a constant hand in the work, and
had found it exceedingly interesting; it involved
inquiries and researches of the most stimulating and
profitable kind. Scholastica was very happy. Her

friend was often absent for many days, during which she knew he was leading the great world's life ; but she had learned that if she patiently waited, the pendulum would swing back, and he would reappear and bury himself in their books and papers and talk. And their talk, you may be sure, was not all technical ; they touched on everything that came into their heads, and Benvolio by no means felt obliged to be silent about those mundane matters as to which a vow of personal ignorance had been taken for his companion. He took her into his poetic confidence, and read her everything he had written since his return from Italy. The more he worked the more he desired to work ; and so, at this time, occupied as he was with editing the Professor's manuscripts, he had never been so productive on his own account. He wrote another drama, on an Italian subject, which was performed with magnificent success ; and this production he discussed with Scholastica scene by scene and speech by speech. He proposed to her to come and see it acted from a covered box, where her seclusion would be complete. She seemed for an instant to feel the force of the temptation ; then she shook her head with a frank

smile, and said it was better not. The play was
dedicated to the Countess, who had suggested the
subject to him in Italy, where it had been imparted
to her, as a family anecdote, by one of her old
princesses. This easy, fruitful, complex life might
have lasted for ever, but for two most regrettable
events. *Might* have lasted I say; you observe I do
not affirm it positively. Scholastica lost her peace
of mind; she was suffering a secret annoyance. She
concealed it as far as she might from her friend,
and with some success; for although he suspected
something and questioned her, she persuaded him
that it was his own fancy. In reality it was no fancy
at all, but the very uncomfortable fact that her
shabby old uncle, the miser, was a terrible thorn in
her side. He had told Benvolio that she might
do as she liked, but he had recently revoked this
amiable concession. He informed her one day, by
means of an illegible note, scrawled with a blunt
pencil, on the back of an old letter, that her beggarly
friend the Poet came to see her altogether too often;
that he was determined she never should marry a
crack-brained rhymester; and that he requested that
before the sacrifice became too painful she would be

so good as to dismiss Mr. Benvolio. This was accompanied by an intimation, more explicit than gracious, that he opened his money-bags only for those who deferred to his incomparable wisdom. Scholastica was poor, and simple, and lonely; but she was proud, for all that, with a shrinking and unexpressed pride of her own, and her uncle's charity, proffered on these terms, became intolerably bitter to her soul. She sent him word that she thanked him for his past liberality, but she would no longer be a charge upon him. She said to herself that she could work; she had a superior education; many women, she knew, supported themselves. She even found something inspiring in the idea of going out into the world of which she knew so little, to seek her fortune. Her great desire, however, was to keep her situation a secret from Benvolio, and to prevent his knowing the sacrifice she was making for him. This it is especially that proves she was proud. It so happened that circumstances made secrecy possible. I don't know whether the Countess had always an idea of marrying Benvolio, but her imperious vanity still suffered from the spectacle of his divided allegiance, and it suggested to her a truly malignant revenge.

A brilliant political mission, to treat of a special
question, was about to be despatched to a neighbouring government, and half a dozen young men of
eminence were to be attached to it. The Countess
had influence at Court, and without saying anything
to Benvolio, she immediately urged his claim to a
post on the ground of his distinguished services to
literature. She pulled her wires so cleverly that in
a very short time she had the pleasure of presenting
him his appointment on a great sheet of parchment,
from which the royal seal dangled by a blue ribbon.
It involved an exile of but a few weeks, and to this
with her eye on the sequel of her project, she was
able to resign herself. Benvolio's imagination took
fire at the thought of spending a month at a foreign
court, in the very hotbed of consummate diplomacy;
this was a phase of experience with which he was as
yet unacquainted. He departed, and no sooner had
he gone than the Countess, at a venture, waited upon
Scholastica. She knew the girl was poor, and she
believed that in spite of her homely virtues she would
not, if the opportunity were placed before her in a
certain light, prove implacably indisposed to better
her fortunes. She knew nothing of the young girl's

contingent expectations from her uncle, and her interference at this juncture was simply a remarkable coincidence. She laid before her a proposal from a certain great lady, whose husband, an eminent general, had just been dubbed governor of an island on the other side of the globe. This lady desired a preceptress for her children; she had heard of Scholastica's merit, and she ventured to hope that she might persuade her to accompany her to the Antipodes and reside in her family. The offer was brilliant; to Scholastica it seemed mysteriously and providentially opportune. Nevertheless she hesitated, and demanded time for reflection; without telling herself why, she wished to wait till Benvolio should return. He wrote her two or three letters, full of the echoes of his brilliant actual life, and without a word about the things that were nearer her own experience. The month elapsed, but he was still absent. Scholastica, who was in correspondence with the governor's wife, delayed her decision from week to week. She had sold her father's manuscripts to a publisher, for a very small sum, and gone, meanwhile, to live in a convent. At last the governor's lady demanded her ultimatum. The poor girl scanned the horizon, and saw no rescuing friend ; Benvolio was still at the court of Illyria ! What she saw was the Countess's fine eyes eagerly watching her over the top of her fan. They seemed to contain a horrible menace, and to hold somehow her happiness at their mercy. Her heart sank ; she gathered up her few possessions and set sail, with her illustrious protectors, for the Antipodes. Shortly after her departure Benvolio returned. He felt a terrible pang of rage and grief when he learned that she had gone ; he went to the Countess, prepared to accuse her of the basest treachery. But she checked his reproaches by arts that she had never gone so far as to use before, and promised him that, if he would trust her, he should never miss that pale-eyed little governess. It can hardly be supposed that he believed her ; but he appears to have been guilty of letting himself be persuaded without belief. For some time after this he almost lived with the Countess. He had, with infinite pains, purchased from his neighbour, the miser, the right of occupancy of the late Professor's apartment. This repulsive proprietor, in spite of his constitutional aversion to rhymesters, had not resisted the financial argument,

and seemed greatly amazed that a poet should
have a dollar to spend. Scholastica had left all
things in their old places, but Benvolio, for the
present, never went into the room. He turned the
key in the door, and kept it in his waistcoat-
pocket, where, while he was with the Countess, his
fingers fumbled with it. Several months rolled by,
and the Countess's promise was not verified. He
missed Scholastica wofully, and missed her more
as time elapsed. He began at last to go to the
old brown room and to try to do some work there.
He only half succeeded in a fashion; it seemed dark
and empty; doubly empty when he remembered what
it might have been. Suddenly he ceased to visit the
Countess; a long time passed without her seeing
him. She met him at another house, and had some
remarkable words with him. She covered him with
reproaches that were doubtless deserved, but he made
her an answer that caused her to open her eyes
and flush, and admit afterward that, for a clever
woman, she had been a great fool. "Don't you see,"
he said, "can't you imagine, that I cared for you
only by contrast? You took the trouble to kill the
contrast, and with it you killed everything else. For

a constancy I prefer *this!*" And he tapped his poetic brow. He never saw the Countess again.

I rather regret now that I said at the beginning of my story that it was not to be a fairy-tale; otherwise I should be at liberty to relate, with harmonious geniality, that if Benvolio missed Scholastica, he missed the Countess also, and led an extremely fretful and unproductive life, until one day he sailed for the Antipodes and brought Scholastica home. After this he began to produce again; only, many people said that his poetry had become dismally dull. But excuse me; I am writing as if it *were* a fairy-tale!

THE END.

LONDON :
R. CLAY, SONS, AND TAYLOR, PRINTERS,
BREAD STREET HILL.

www.ingramcontent.com/pod-product-compliance
Lightning Source LLC
Chambersburg PA
CBHW030805020726

47499CB00006B/1775